SECRET PASSIONS

JILL SANDERS

GRAYTON

To women everywhere
who have been oppressed.
There is hope.

SUMMARY

Sandi has escaped her old life. She's shed her hijab and her family obligations to start a new life, alone. It's been five years since she first stepped foot in America to save her life. She's earned enough money to live comfortably, thanks to her artwork. Just when she finally feels like she can start to relax and not jump at shadows, her past returns, hot on her heels. Now she must trust the man who saved her years ago and ask him to do it once again.

Mitch risked it all to bring the young girl to America years ago. And when she shows up at his door in the middle of the night all grown up, he'll do everything he can to help her again. Dodging her past has gotten a lot harder this time, but they might survive—if he can keep his hands off her.

PROLOGUE

The young girl sat huddled against the cold metal of the ship. She shivered, not from the lack of warmth, but out of fear. She'd never left her home before. She'd never been on her own. Now she looked around the large room at all the men surrounding her and realized she'd never been around so many people of the opposite sex. Her life had been full of gardens, women, family, and rules.

Reaching up, she felt her short hair, tight against her scalp. Gone was the long flowing soft length that reached all the way to the bottom of her back. It would grow back, but she still missed the weight of it. She looked down at the strange clothes; she was still trying to get used to wearing pants. Dressed as a young soldier, she realized she fit right in with all the men surrounding her. It was the first time she'd ever wore pants or boots. I guess there was quite a list of firsts for her now.

"Are you okay?" the large man asked her. His name was Ethan, and she owed him more than she could ever repay. He'd told her he was just the delivery man, that it was Mitchell Kovich whom she owed. She nodded her head at him, and he crossed his muscular arms behind his head and closed his eyes as he laid back on the cot.

She sat on her bunk, afraid to close her eyes, as the large vessel slowly made its way towards her freedom.

Her mind conjured up images of Mitchell Kovich. He'd be tall, blonde, and very handsome. She'd spoken to him on the phone several times and knew his voice was smooth and rich sounding. She enjoyed his American accent and had even privately worked on getting rid of her own Eastern dialect. In her mind, she practiced during the long trip. At least when she wasn't thinking about her new life or Mitchell Kovich.

Sandi threw down her brush and glared at the canvas in front of her. There were drops of every color of paint on the floorboards that creaked under her feet. The old wood showed the true meaning behind her art. She'd once thought to rip it up, board by board, and frame it. Now, as she stood back and looked at the piece she had just completed, she started to smile slowly.

The painting was a mix of bright colors and when she unfocused her eyes, she could just make out the memory in her head. She was spun back in time to a place full of sights and sounds. Large trees hung overhead, leaves blew in the warm wind. The laughter of children could be heard, and the scent of spices and home filled her nose.

Hearing a fog horn bellow in the distance brought her back to the present. She looked around the large room that had been her sanctuary for the last two years. The large windows overlooked the New York harbor. The loft was one of the most expensive in the waterfront building. She'd worked hard for the comforts she had, and she paid dearly to get where she was. After meticulously cleaning her brushes and pallet, she walked over to the glass, looked down, and felt a sense of comfort. People walked on the streets below. She was ten stories up, so she couldn't make out their faces or their expressions as they passed by. Happy, excited, relaxed, tense, nervous, stressed, upset, sad, and scared—every person's emotions looked the same this high up.

Turning back to the room, she looked around. Here there was an obvious void of color. She'd chosen to leave this room white. Walls, furniture, everything was clean and clear. In this room, her art was all the color she needed. Leaving her latest masterpiece to dry, she walked from the room into her living area.

The absence of furniture here was her choice. One large couch sat in the middle of the floor. A small flat screen television hung on the opposite wall. This room was smaller than the other, but here she had splashes of color. Dark purple pillows on the couch. Green and blue jars sitting in the windowsills. Royal red tapestries hung on several walls, each with its own unique story to tell.

She enjoyed collecting these small things on her outings into the city. She didn't know why the colored bottles called to her, but she couldn't seem to resist their charm when she found one. The light in her windows always shown through them, casting different hues onto her walls. As for the tapestries, well, she had a weakness for art and to her, true art was woven centuries ago. She could just sit there and stare at the different works, making up the lives of the person who had painstakingly taken their time to create the masterpieces.

She walked into the kitchen and started to make herself a cup of coffee, a sin she started shortly after her trek across the world. The taste was nothing compared to the tea she had grown up drinking, but she had purposely decided to end all her old habits when she had stepped foot on American soil five years ago. She stopped and looked down at her hands. Five years ago. Had it really been only five years?

She placed the small container in her new toy that made her coffee just right. The single-cup coffee maker was something she had splurged on. Its brightly lit screen showed so many different settings, and it even told her the temperature of her coffee.

Now, as she began to smell the hazelnut coffee brewing, she leaned back on the marble countertop and enjoyed the peace and quiet of her life. She didn't mind living alone; actually, she enjoyed having the space to herself. When she'd first arrived, she had lived in a small apartment with three other women, all of whom had been smuggled out of various countries. Protection had been instilled into her mind that first year. The shelter she had lived in trained her how to live on her own. She took self-defense classes for the first two years. She learned how to pay her bills, how to grocery shop, even how to interact with other people without giving up vital information about who she was or where she was from.

She owed everything she was now to a group of people, and she didn't think she could ever repay them. Since her art had taken off almost two years ago, she had slowly been shuffling a big chunk of her income back into the shelter, helping the group of people who had helped her start her new life. She had also found a women's shelter in her home town back in India that she donated to. Someday she hoped to visit it and see firsthand the wonderful work they did to protect young girls and women from falling into the same dangers she had.

There were still a few people she had yet to make contact with since her arrival, three men in particular that she owed most of her gratitude to. It was strange to think that men she knew and loved had caused all her problems, and yet it was men whom she hadn't even met that had bailed her out of it all.

She could still remember seeing the first man's face as he hung upside down from her father's balcony. It had been so dark, for a second, she had thought he was a man of color. Then the light had reflected off the paint he had used to darken his skin. She had thought he was there to kill her. She had prepared herself for the worst and was relieved that her suffering would be over quickly. When he had quietly told her to come with him, and that he was there to take her to America, she knew she had been saved.

The long trip over here was something she would never forget. Neither was the first face she saw when she had woken that first morning. She'd woken to low voices and realized she was no longer in the small cot on the boat, but instead she was lying on a soft couch. When she had opened her eyes, she had seen the most beautiful man she'd ever laid eyes on. Of course, at eighteen she had only ever seen three men before: her father, her uncle, and her cousin. Though she could hardly call her cousin a man since he was just a year older than her.

Just then her phone rang, causing her to jump. She realized her coffee was done and getting cold. She really had to stop daydreaming so much. She supposed it was a side effect of being an artist. Rushing over to the phone, she checked the caller ID and saw her agent's name. Eve Taylor was someone she had known and come to trust over the last three years. Eve worked for The Kovich and Edwards Agency, which was the company passed to her by Ric Derby to help her sell her art, when she had started her journey over five years ago. Ric was one of the other men she owed everything to, especially since Ric and his wife Roberta had almost been killed by her uncle five years ago.

"Hello?" She smiled, knowing the simple task of

answering the phone was something she was now allowed to do. She was no longer controlled to a point where she couldn't do simple things.

"Hi, it's Eve. I'm calling to see if you have the last two pieces ready for the show this weekend." Eve said, sounding a little eager.

"Yes, actually I just finished the last watercolor. Would you like me to bring them over later today?" Sandi leaned on the counter and held the phone tight.

"Oh wonderful, how about we meet somewhere for lunch? I've been meaning to chat with you about another show. This way we can write lunch off and charge it to the corporate card." She listened to Eve laugh, then she heard her cover the phone and speak with someone else. The muffled voices were obviously arguing about something. Sandi knew from her past experience that Eve and her boss, Carter Edwards, didn't always see eye to eye.

"I'm sorry, as I was saying, before I was *rudely* interrupted, how about we meet down at that cafe just down the street from your place? What was the name of it again?" Sandi could hear Eve digging through some paperwork.

"Hell's Kitchen Cafe?" She suggested.

"Yes, that's the one. They have such wonderful soup. How about we meet there in ... two hours?" Eve asked.

Sandi looked over to the clock on her stove and saw that it was a quarter past ten. She hadn't even made it to bed last night. Yet somehow, she was totally refreshed, and she hadn't even had her coffee yet.

"That sounds great. I'll see you then." After hanging up with Eve, Sandi took her lukewarm coffee and started up her long staircase towards her room. Drinking her coffee on the way, she felt energy slowly flowing back into her. After grabbing a quick shower, she donned a simple brown skirt and a tank top made of red silk. She tied her long dark hair up in a braid and smiled when she noticed how light it was getting. She'd spent quite a lot of her summer outside in the park. She enjoyed bringing her easel and working in the sun. Her skin even had an extra glow to it. For her heritage, she was oddly pale.

She had heard a story once as a child that her great-great-grandmother was Anglo-Saxon and the woman had been brought over to India on a slave ship. Her great-great-grandmother's yellow hair and pale skin had caught the eye of her wealthy great-great-grandfather and she had been quickly bought up and taken in as his fifth wife. Sandi had been told when she was younger that she was cursed with her great-great-grandmother's pale skin and had lighter hair to show for it. Even her eyes were a shade lighter than her father's and mother's eyes. Her hair had a slight wave to it. It all helped her feel more like she fit in here in America and she was thankful. She had spent the first year in America learning to talk without a strong accent. She had even mastered speaking with several different accents, just to test the waters out.

Her second year here she had taken to talking with a quaint British accent. Everyone she talked to asked which part of England she was from. She enjoyed making up different stories to tell everyone she met.

The next year, after she had moved several times, she had tried an Australian accent. That one was not only fun but very addictive. She found that she tended to revert back to it when she was tired or not paying attention.

After she had moved into this building, however, she had finally settled on a simple cross between a New York and European accent. It had been three years now and she felt like she could finally stop worrying about slipping back into her native tongue. It had taken her longer to learn the written language than the spoken words. Of course, it didn't help that she had barely learned how to write in her native Hindi. Her mother had tried to teach her the basics as a child, but since she wasn't allowed to attend school, she hadn't given it much thought. Since her mother had been very short on patience, Sandi had ended up drawing most of the time.

She'd also changed her looks while she'd been here. When she'd first arrived, her hair had been cut so short. It had grown fast, and she'd tried many new styles since she'd always had longer hair growing up. She'd experimented with adding some temporary colors, decided it was fun, and so kept doing it. She currently had a few deep red streaks throughout her hair. She'd settled on keeping her hair shoulder length, and she enjoyed the slight curl that it had at this length.

Walking into her art room, she checked that her new piece was dry. Knowing she still had some time before she had to meet Eve, she took her time pulling down the other five pieces she would carry the four blocks to the cafe.

A while later, as she was juggling the large portfolio bag that was hanging from her shoulder and trying to lock her front door, she heard the door behind her open.

Sandi jumped a little and twisted to see her neighbor Mrs. Bernstein standing in her doorway in her long bathrobe. "Oh, it's you. I thought you might be the delivery boy. He's always late on Tuesdays." The older woman said, peeking out the locked door.

"Hello, Mrs. Bernstein. How are you doing today?" Sandi smiled.

"Oh, you know, no complaints from me. Well, don't you look pretty today. You wouldn't by chance be meeting a young man for lunch now, would you?" The door opened a little more as she spoke.

Sandi chuckled. Mrs. Bernstein was a sweet meddler, always asking her if she was meeting a boy. She had even tried once to set her up with her grandson, who was only eighteen.

"No, I'm just meeting my agent. I'm giving her the last of my paintings for that show I was telling you about." Sandi patted her portfolio bag.

"Oh, that's lovely dear. You have such a wonderful talent. Well, I won't keep you long. You be safe out there." The door started to close before she was done speaking.

"I will." Sandi finished locking her door and swung her bag over her left shoulder as the older woman glanced down the hall with a worried look and then closed her door quickly. Sandi could hear the multiple locks engage as the woman shut herself back into the apartment that was her entire world.

In all the time Sandi had lived there, she'd never seen Mrs. Bernstein step foot outside her doorway. She doubted the woman had even walked to the elevators in the last three years. Carrying her heavy bag, she headed out to her meeting.

Half an hour later she walked up to the small cafe and smiled when she noticed Eve sitting outside at a table under a large green umbrella. Eve waved to her as she approached. Eve Taylor was easily the prettiest woman Sandi had ever seen. Her olive skin and large hazel eyes were things Sandi had always dreamed of having. Not to mention her rich chestnut hair and long curvy figure. Sandi knew there was some Italian in Eve's family, she just didn't know how far back it went.

"There you are. I was ready to send out a search party," Eve joked.

Setting down her heavy portfolio bag, she gave Eve a light hug and sat down. "I should have taken a taxi, but it is such a nice day I decided to walk."

"First, let me have a look at these." Sandi waited as Eve

took out her paintings and looked at them one by one. The waiter came and took Sandi's order as Eve studied the canvases.

"These are beautiful. I don't know how you do it, but every new piece is something I fully desire. I want to keep them all to myself." Eve smiled over the table at her, and finally Sandi felt the tension leave her shoulders. Why did she still find it hard to accept that her art was good? Not until she heard it from someone else, did she fully believe in herself. It was the small doubt that played in the back of her mind that always drove her to perfection. Maybe it was a good thing that she was so driven to please others. It probably helped her art to be the finest. Her art, Eve and Carter often told her was selling like hot cakes in art galleries around the world. Of course, she sold everything under the pseudonym Samantha Rain. She couldn't afford to be found.

"Now, tell me about this new project and what kind of art you'll need for it." She said, then sat back and listened to Eve talk about a charity auction for terminally ill children, she couldn't help but thinking about her own future. Would she ever have children of her own? She knew she would have to find a husband first. A frown formed on her face, and she quickly wiped it away before Eve could ask about it. She didn't think too highly of men. She just didn't trust them. But she did want a family and children. She had always wanted that as much as she had wanted to paint.

"You're not really listening to me are you?" Eve leaned her chin in her hands and smiled at her.

Sandi laughed. "I'm sorry. You were talking about children which got me thinking about having a few myself. I'd be happy to provide several pieces for the auction. When do you need them by?"

Less than an hour later Sandi was walking back to her apartment, her empty portfolio bag slung over her shoulder.

She was once again caught up in daydreaming about children and her future. She wondered what kind of man could ever draw her in so much that she could drop the shield she had built over the last five years. Then a face popped into her mind. Sea-green eyes full of concern, sandy blond hair that looked soft and inviting, a chin chiseled out of stone with a cute little cleft in it.

With her mind on the man of her dreams, she would have walked right up to her building if it hadn't been for the kid on a skateboard. She wasn't focusing on her surroundings until the young boy zipped by, almost knocking her down. Then her eyes focused, and one of the first things she noticed was the dark sedan parked across from her building in the loading zone. Her steps faltered, and she quickly rushed to the corner and peeked out from behind the newsstand that sat there.

She watched as two men got out of the car and her heart sank. She knew the penalty for what she'd done five years ago was death. Her mind raced. How had they found her? What was she going to do now? She knew one thing for sure; there was no way she could ever go home again. Her life would have to start over, again.

MITCHELL KOVICH TOOK another breath and pulled himself up for the last time. Slowly releasing his breath, he swung back down. Once his feet were back on the ground, he let his arms fall and felt himself sway with fatigue. He was getting too old for this shit. Okay, maybe not too old; he was only a few months shy of his thirty-second birthday, but he started thinking of cutting back to one-hundred pull-ups a day instead of one-fifty.

His arms screamed, his back screamed, and the rest of

him, well... He closed his eyes and rolled his shoulders. Having a home gym had always been a blessing. This way no one could tell if you cut back a little. But he hadn't counted on the guilty feeling he got when he didn't do his full sets. Besides, he always felt better after he showered and rested.

Draping his towel over his shoulders, he made his way upstairs to shower. The place felt empty since Suzanne had moved out three months ago. He didn't mind it, though, considering she was now snuggled up with some other woman. Yeah, it had been a blow, walking in and seeing the two women locked together. His first thought had been excitement; after all, he was a man. But when the two of them had jumped apart and quickly covered themselves, he had known it wasn't an early birthday present as he'd first thought.

Later that evening, she had mumbled through an apology and tried to explain how she felt before packing her things and leaving for good. It was just so hard to be mad at the other person when you felt inadequate yourself. He'd spent the first month wondering what he'd done wrong. Then he'd graduated to anger. How had he not seen this coming? Suzanne was always more comfortable around women, she was always very hands-on with them and had, in the last year of their relationship, pulled farther away from him. Hell, he and Suzanne hadn't even had sex for almost three months before he'd walked in on the two women. Which got him thinking about how horny he was now. He wanted a woman. No, he needed a woman. But he didn't want to put himself out there again. Not like he'd done with Suzanne. He'd spent almost two years building their friendship and relationship to what it was before she'd cheated. When he first met her, they'd had to work on the physical part, which should have been the first clue to him to stop then. It had seemed like she'd kept putting on the brakes when they'd dated. When they'd finally had sex, it had been ... well, awkward was the best word. He'd never had issues like that before. But he'd fallen for her, and he'd tried very hard to make their relationship work. And it had seemed to work for a while.

He was at a point in his life now when even his buddies were trying to hook him up. Carter, his business partner of seven years and best friend since grade school, was always pointing out women to him. They had started the Kovich & Edward Agency together and the agency had grown to new heights. They now held accounts ranging from high-paid artists and actors, and even some very predominate sports figures.

Another friend had told him that he should get right back on the horse, but after the first couple of weeks, they got his hint that he just wanted to be left alone. In Mitchell's mind, it was too soon to try and trust someone in a relationship again.

He was half-way through a cold shower when his doorbell went off. It didn't just go off, someone had their damned finger holding it down. Jumping from the shower, he grabbed a towel off the counter, quickly wrapped it around his hips, and set off to berate whoever didn't know how to ring a damned doorbell. Thinking it would be Carter, he swung open the door without looking through the peephole.

"What the hell..." he was shocked to see the most beautiful woman he'd ever laid eyes on standing there still holding the bell. Her dark hair hung in a braid that was a little frazzled. Her top was falling off of her frail looking shoulder. Her dark skin shone. Her eyes caught his attention. Their deepness spoke so much more than any he'd ever seen.

His mouth was still open, ready to yell and cuss out whoever had interrupted his "me time".

"Oh, good. You *are* home," the woman said with a sexy accent. Then she walked right past him into his living room.

CHAPTER 2

Sandi walked into the large living room, tossed down her empty portfolio bag, and tried not to show her emotions. To say that she was shocked when Mitchell opened the door wearing nothing, but a small white towel would have been an understatement. She didn't have any experience with men. She hadn't even seen a man's chest before, let alone seeing one half-naked, dripping wet, and absolutely yummy. His sandy blond hair was curled and dripping water down his tan neck. She saw with delight that he had a slight dusting of sandy colored hair on his chest and arms. His legs had it, too, and she noticed his bare feet as he dripped water on the tile floor.

Turning, she walked across the room and stopped just short of the large bay windows in his place. Looking out at the darkness that surrounded his street, she strained her eyes, looking for a dark sedan. Pulling the curtains closed quickly, she turned when she realized the room was quiet.

He stood across the room, leaning against the back of the door, his arms casually draped over his chest, watching her.

He had a small frown on his lips, and she could see a small crease between his eyebrows.

"Well?" she looked at him and started walking towards him. "Don't just stand there. Lock that door."

His eyebrows shot up in question. "Although I do appreciate a good surprise, I'd like to know who sent you over here first."

She stopped halfway across the room. "What? You don't remember me?"

"Should I? Wait, don't tell me. This is some sort of payback from Carter, isn't it?" He uncrossed his arms and started walking towards her. "Listen, I only mentioned Eve the other night because... well... It's none of your damn business." He waved his arms about, then stopped and turned back towards her, a shocked look on his face. "Oh, God! He didn't pay you anything did he?"

"What *are* you talking about?" Since he hadn't done it himself, she walked over and flipped his deadbolt. Then she turned, walked back to his couch, and sat down on the soft cushions. She leaned over and pulled off her heels and started rubbing her feet. Walking over fifty blocks in those heels had been hell, and she was relieved to be out of her stylish shoes.

She stopped rubbing her feet and looked up at him when the room got really quiet. She waited for him to respond. He was watching her like he was trying to figure out what to do next.

"Well?" She asked again as she leaned back against the couch. It had taken most of the day to figure out what she was going to do after spotting the men outside her apartment. She'd wandered around for the first few hours. Then, with a plan firmly planted in her mind, she'd headed the fifty-odd blocks to Mitchell's place. She could have used a cab, but she was low on cash and didn't think she should use her credit cards. At this point, she needed to be very safe.

"If Carter didn't send you it must have been Trent. I've told these guys to leave me alone..." He started walking around the room waving his hands as he talked. She closed her eyes and released a sigh. How could a man be so confusing? Maybe her head was a little dull from everything that had happened to her in the last four hours. Maybe she needed some food. After all, she hadn't eaten anything since her meeting with Eve. Plus, she'd walked halfway across Manhattan. In heels no less! Her mind refused to focus, and she found the sound of Mitchell's voice soothing.

Then she jumped at the sound of his telephone ringing. She was up, standing at the edge of the couch, fear in her eyes as he watched her.

"Easy." He said, holding his hands out. "It's just my phone." He walked over, noticed the name on his phone, and answered it. "Hello, Carter."

"You? Did you get the gift I sent over?" Carter answered. Mitchell looked across the room at the woman. She had walked back to the window and was looking out through the closed blinds.

"It was you!" he whispered into the phone. "What were you thinking, man? I can't believe you'd do something like this." Mitch walked into the other room, keeping his eyes on the girl.

"Yeah," his friend chuckled. "I thought you'd get a laugh out of it. Have you used it yet?"

Mitchell's mind instantly jumped to an image of the woman underneath him. "What? Are you insane? I can't believe you'd do something like this," he repeated.

"Easy, bro. It's just a stupid indoor basketball hoop. Nobody's twisting your arm to use it. I thought you'd hang it on the edge of your balcony and get some use out of it. Besides, you could always return it. They should have given you the receipt when they delivered it."

Just then, Mitchell's doorbell rang. He watched as the young woman jumped away from the windows. He started back into the room, still holding the phone to his ear. "I'll call you right back."

When Mitch reached his front door, he watched the woman frantically look around. When he started opening the door, she yelled at him in a hushed tone. "Don't open that!"

He stopped and looked at her. She *was* running from someone. The fear was written all over her face. He actually saw her shoulders shaking.

He stopped and looked out the peephole. "Easy, it's just a delivery. I was expecting it." He swung open his door and sure enough, two young men stood there with a large box.

Five minutes later, Mitch closed his door and turned back to the room. She'd sat back down on the couch, but this time looked more alert.

"Listen, let me go put some clothes on, then you can tell me what kind of trouble you're in." He started walking towards his stairs. "You aren't going to steal anything while I'm up there, are you?"

She looked shocked and offended, which answered his question. "Good. I'll be right back." He jogged up the stairs without waiting for a reply.

Ten minutes later, he walked out onto his balcony and looked down. She was on his couch, her head slightly tilted back, and her eyes closed. Her feet were tucked up under her, and he was pretty sure she was fast asleep. He quietly went down the stairs and walked closer to get a good look at her. His mind sharpened. She'd looked tired when she'd walked in, he just hadn't noticed. Instead, his hormones had been thrust into overdrive. He'd been around pretty women before—Suzanne had been one of them—but when this woman had walked in, his brain had felt like it had just gone on vacation.

Of course, he'd jumped to conclusions. But there just wasn't any easy explanation for why a very attractive woman would barge into his home and lock herself in. How did she know that he wasn't some sort of rapist or serial killer? Had she picked his place by accident? Was someone chasing her? She had asked him to lock his door. No doubt someone was following her, and she was in trouble, which would account for her being jumpy.

Standing over her, looking down at her dark head, he noticed several things about her. Her hair had red streaks running through it, and in spots, it had lightened like the sun had bleached it. Her skin was darker, probably due to some Indian or middle-eastern heritage. He guessed that she had some European lineage in her, too, due to the lighter skin and some of her features. She'd spoken with an English accent as well. She was dressed in a simple yet stylish long skirt with a classy, colorful top. Her shoes, which were lying on the floor, looked very expensive. Long gold earrings hung in her ears, and she had on a simple gold necklace that matched. She didn't wear any rings, and he didn't see a purse anywhere. He thought about shaking her awake, but when he moved to get closer, her eyes opened, and he realized how dark they were. Like his coffee in the morning, rich and dark.

"I think we need to talk," he said, and she nodded her head and sat up, placing her hands in her lap. He walked over and sat in the chair across from his couch. "Just who is it you're running from?"

"My father and my cousin." She had a funny look on her

face, and he was sure she was trying to figure something out in her head.

"What's your name?" He leaned forward, his arms resting on his knees.

"Sandi." She watched his face for a response.

"Sandi, what?" He asked.

"You don't remember me?" she twisted her skirt between her fingers.

"No? Should I?" He leaned back.

She watched him, quietly. Finally, after a minute had passed, she got up from the couch and started pacing his living room. Her arms were crossed in front of her.

"I guess it was a mistake coming here. It's been five years. I should have known you wouldn't remember me. You probably haven't even thought about me once since that night." She glanced at the door.

His mind quickly spun to what he was doing five years ago. To whom he was doing it with. Surely, he would have remembered a night with this beautiful woman.

"I just didn't know who else to turn to." She turned back to him and he could see she was holding back tears. "I tried to find Ethan, but I didn't know where to start. I thought maybe you'd know where he was, and what I should do now that they've found me." She started rubbing her forehead with her fingers.

"Take it easy." He stood and walked over to her. He could see by the look on her face that she was slowly working herself into a state of hysterics. "Sandi?" He took her slim shoulders into his hands and waited for her to look back into his eyes. "Why don't you sit down? I'll get you a glass of water and you can start from the beginning."

She took a deep breath and closed her eyes. Taking another, she opened them and nodded her agreement.

He walked into the kitchen and poured her a cold glass of

water. While he was there, he picked up the phone and punched in Ethan Knight's new cell number. When it went to voicemail, he left a short message.

"Hey, Ethan. Mitch here. I've got a young girl, Sandi, in my apartment. She's in bad trouble and apparently, you helped her out before. Give me a call when you get this message. It looks like I'll need your help again on this one."

He walked back into the room and sat as she took a deep drink of the water.

"I guess I was thirsty. I hadn't had anything to eat or drink since my meeting with Eve."

"Eve Taylor?" he asked, and she nodded her head.

"Yes." She took another deep breath. "Five years ago, last spring, you and Ethan helped me escape my family in Puri. I'm Sannidhi Rangan." She waited and watched him for a response.

He vaguely remembered helping a young Indian artist. It was during his drinking days, so most of what had transpired in those three years was a blur. "Okay, and now you say that your father and cousin have found you?'

She nodded and looked down at the glass she was still holding in her hands.

He thought about the consequences of what she'd done. He knew the horror stories of honor killings that still happened today. Family members killed young women for far less than what Sandi had done, what he'd helped her do five years ago. "Are you sure?" He asked.

"They're outside my apartment, I can't go back there. I didn't know who else to trust." Her voice sounded strained.

"You work with Eve?" He asked.

"Yes, Kovich & Edward Agency has been selling my artwork under my pseudonym. I've only dealt with Eve since signing on three years ago. Ric thought that the fewer people I dealt with, the better." She said quickly.

Upon hearing Ric's name, it all became clearer to him. Mitchell had almost gotten Ric Derby and his new wife killed over this young artist, Sannidhi, or Sandi, as she liked to be called. She had been a seventeen-year-old prodigy. Her hands tied by her government and her family, she was destined to marry someone she didn't know. She'd called him late one night while he'd been in a drunken stupor and had begged for his help. He'd hung up and called his old friend Ethan and had asked him to handle it all.

Weeks later he'd found out that the girl's family was searching for her. Apparently, they had money, big money, and he'd pissed off a lot of people. At that point, he was still unsure where Ethan and the girl were. All he knew was that Ethan had called and told him they'd meet him in three weeks.

He'd tried to tell Ric about the mess he'd gotten himself in but had been too scared to break his friend's trust. That decision had almost cost his friend his life. Actually, the day he'd visited Ric and his new wife, Roberta, at the hospital after she'd been shot was the last day he'd had a drink. Over five years of being sober, and he'd never once thought about picking up the bottle. The image of Ric's wife lying in the hospital bed after the bullet, which had been close to her heart, had been removed had cured him of his past indiscretions.

He looked across the room at Sandi and tried to remember meeting her for the first time. She'd been dressed in dark military fatigues, her face and body covered by the large clothes, a disguise. Her dark hair had been cut short, military short, showing most of her scalp through it. Ethan's plan to hide her in plain sight was to dress her as a young male Marine. She had looked the part at the time.

"Sandi?" He was shocked. The girl he remembered

meeting that night was nothing like the woman who sat before him now. She smiled a little and nodded her head.

Remembering the family she'd come from—the determination they had to find her, how they would stop at nothing to get their hands on her—he ran his hands through his hair and realized just how screwed they were.

itchell tried to reach Ethan three more times before he finally gave up. His friend was just not answering. He was probably deep undercover somewhere.

Mitch was pacing the living room floor, while Sandi sat on the couch looking tired and frazzled.

"Mitchell? I hate to ask, but do you by chance have anything I could eat?" She looked apologetic.

He stopped and looked at her. What kind of host was he? She'd obviously been tired when she had arrived, and all he'd done so far was offer her a glass of water and ogle her, thinking that she was hired to please him.

"I'm sorry, you must be starved. Stay right here, and I'll fix something for you." He rushed across the room and decided to make a quick pot of stir-fry.

Cooking was something he always did when he needed to work something out. He barely noticed when she walked across the room and sat at the bar, watching him. He was chopping the onions when she came close to him.

"Here, I can do this." She leaned on the countertop to take

the knife from his hands and he smelled her hair. It smelled of jasmine and he wanted to lean closer to enjoy even more of her.

"Tell me what you've been doing since I last saw you. How have you enjoyed America? You obviously lost the thick accent." He moved over to stir the rice.

"Oh, I still have it when I want to," she said with her native accent. He smiled down at her. "I've also picked up a few others along the way," she said easily in another, more common accent, sounding like she was from the Bronx.

"You have a talent for it." He picked up his grandfather's Irish brogue. They smiled at each other.

"Well, I've been painting, and Eve has been doing a wonderful job making me and you quite a lot of money. Other than that, I've been enjoying my freedom." She shrugged her shoulders, then moved over and tossed the onions into the pan. "What else can I chop?"

"There are some green peppers and some celery in the refrigerator." He nodded towards the fridge.

They made a good team in the kitchen. In no time his place smelled of rich food, and by the time they sat down to eat, they were both laughing. Mitchell realized as he bit into the spicy food that for the first time since his break up with Suzanne, he had thoroughly enjoyed the company of another woman.

SANDI HELPED him clear up after dinner. She felt bad for putting him out, for making him entertain her, but she saw no other options. She just couldn't afford to trust anyone. After all, she still had to figure out how her father had found her. She was living under a different name, keeping her head down, not causing herself to stand out.

"Mitch, I need to find out how my family found me." She said.

They were sitting back in the living room. Her feet were tucked back underneath her, and she was enjoying a cup of coffee he'd made.

"What do you mean?" he asked.

"Well, I've thought a lot about this since seeing my father outside my apartment. How did he find me? It's not like I've gone around shouting out who I am. I don't use my real name, even my rent and credit cards are under the name Ethan gave me five years ago. I thought at first that I had slipped up somehow. But when I was walking over here, I realized there is no way my family could have found me, except through Kovich & Edward Agency." She sat looking at him.

"Wait, what are you saying? That I would have..." he started.

"Oh, no! Not you." She broke in, quickly.

"If not me, then I guess I don't understand what you're saying." He waited, looking at her.

She took a deep breath and leaned back into the couch. "Well, it makes sense. If my father had tracked your agency down through your connection with Ric Derby—after all, as far as my family knows he is the one that brought me to America—all it would take is someone there confirming a woman fitting my description had signed with you."

"But you said you only worked with Eve. She's worked with our company for over two years and I've known her a lot longer than that. There is no way she would ever break our strict confidentiality agreement." He shook his head.

"I never thought it was her. I just don't know how else they would have found me." She rubbed her forehead again and could feel the fatigue setting in.

He looked at her for a few seconds, then said. "Why don't

you go on up and take a nice shower and wash away your problems for the night. You can take the guest room. There are some of Suzanne's, my ex's, clothes in one of the drawers. She was a lot taller than you, but maybe you can find something to fit into. Don't worry about it tonight. I'm sure Ethan will call any time, and he'll figure out what to do next. But for now, you're safe.

She looked across the room and knew she was safe. She'd only truly felt safe in the presence of two men before: Ethan and Mitchell.

Once she was up in his guest room, she remembered staying there that first night, five years ago. Someone had redecorated the room since her last visit. Probably the ex he'd mentioned, Suzanne. She looked through the drawers and wondered what kind of woman had let Mitch slip through her fingers.

That was one thing she just couldn't put her finger on in this country. If she had found a man like Mitch and was lucky enough to be with him, there was nothing she would do to lose him. Maybe that was the problem. Maybe this Suzanne hadn't wanted the relationship. She couldn't imagine Mitch cheating on a woman he was seeing. She didn't know or have a lot of experience with men, but she'd watched enough television since arriving to know how to read a man's character.

She found a small pair of gym shorts and a t-shirt that could easily flow to her knees and took them into the bathroom attached to her room. Turning on the shower, she turned the water to the right temperature and slowly peeled off her own clothes. It felt like she'd hiked across Manhattan in them, and she realized she felt dusty and sweaty. Stepping into the warm water, she was thankful to see a bottle of shampoo and conditioner on the small shelf.

Taking her time, she slowly let the dirt from the day wash

off her while her mind ran over her options. She knew she couldn't hide out at his place for long. After all, if they had found her, they already knew about the connection with Mitchell. She did feel like she was safe for the night but thought it best that she move on tomorrow. She still hadn't thought through exactly where she was going to go.

After her shower, she crawled into the large bed and tried to shut down her mind for the night, but the past found its way into her dreams.

"Pitā, Pitā!" The little girl ran through the large gardens as if floating. Her long brown hair was neatly tied up with silk scarf, which covered most of her head. Brightly colored silk flowed around most of her little body. She cried for her father as she ran through the large glass doors, down the shiny tile hallway, and straight into her father's waiting arms. When she looked up at her father, he smiled with kind eyes.

"What is it, bēṭī? Why are you crying so, my little pālatū?"

She loved being called "pet." It made her feel special that her father had chosen such an endearment for her. She looked up at him through watery eyes.

His face was always something of a comfort to her. His dark skin showed signs of his age around his eyes and mouth. His hair was thick and dark, and she loved running her fingers through it when he comforted her.

"Pitā, why do I have to get married?" she used her best pout and looked into his dark eyes as a tear slipped down her chubby cheek.

"Now, pālatū, we've talked about this. You are not getting married, today."

"Yes, I know, but why do I have to pretend to get married?"

"Sannidhi, this is a great honor. The Mahabir family has chosen you for their son, Ishat. Besides, you will like him. He loves art like you do."

Her little face pouted up more. She didn't like the idea of fake marrying anyone. Especially a boy. She wasn't around boys often. In fact, her father was the only man she'd ever been around. She looked around the room and realized for the first time that it was filled with men. They were guests for the special event, all dressed in brightly colored dhotis, each a beautiful shade of red, much like her own clothing.

Just then her father looked up and smiled. "Go with your mām. There is little time left before the ceremony."

She held onto her father's neck for just another second, then let go as he set her back on the ground. She left the room and walked beside her mother back through the large garden filled with flowers of every color and large stone statues until they reached her rooms.

Here there were other women dressed much like she was, women who had always been there to serve her no matter what her need. Her mother spoke harsh words to her, scolding her for running off to her father. She looked down at her colored hands, which were decorated in Henna, especially for the day's special events.

"I'm sorry, mām. I won't run away again." She looked into her *mother's young smiling face. "Now, turn and look at yourself. Look at how beautiful you look on your special day."*

When Sandi turned and looked at the large walled mirror, instead of seeing a young girl of the age of seven, she saw a full-grown woman. And instead of just her engagement party, it was the day of her wedding. She would no longer belong to herself. Instead, she would be a slave to her husband's family. To bear as many children as he wished, to work, clean, and cook for him and his family. She looked at herself in the mirror and her image slowly transformed in front of her eyes. Wrinkles started forming around her eyes and mouth, her hair turned a light shade until finally, it was full of gray, and now there were too many wrinkles on her face to recognize the child she had been a few minutes before. Her life was over before she had even begun to live.

She woke with a start and looked around the room. When she noticed a silhouette of a man standing in the open doorway, she screamed.

"EASY, it's just me. You were having a bad dream." He watched her relax back against the pillows.

"I'm sorry if I woke you." She sat up a little and he could see the large white t-shirt she wore was one of his.

"I was just passing by when I heard you. I didn't mean to startle you." He took a step into the room.

"It's fine. I guess with everything that happened today, I should have known the dream would follow." She rubbed her forehead with her fingers.

"I could get you a glass of water?" He started to walk towards the bathroom.

"No, that's okay. I'm fine, really." She looked at him and he couldn't help it, he crossed the room and sat on the edge of the bed.

"I've been doing some thinking. I'd like to do some research on your family. Just to see if there is anything we can do to get them off your back. If that's okay with you?" He waited for an answer. He could tell she was thinking about it.

Finally, she asked. "Why? What difference do you think it will make?"

"I'm not sure, but if there is one thing I've learned in my line of business, it's that everyone has a weak point. Maybe there is something further we can learn about your family. Something that will tilt their decisions about you in your favor." He said.

"At this point, I'm willing to try anything." She leaned her head back against the padded headboard, and he noticed that she looked very tired.

"I'll let you get some more rest. We can finish talking about it in the morning." He got up and turned to leave.

"Mitchell?" She asked before he got to the door.

He turned back to her, his hand on the doorknob. "Yes?"

"Thank you for not turning me away. Thank you for sticking your neck out five years ago to save a girl halfway around the world whom you had never met. I know I didn't say it back then when I first met you. I was a different person then. I just wanted you to know that I'm grateful to you. I owe you more than I could ever repay."

He was floored. He didn't quite know how to respond. He felt his throat close up a little and felt a tightness in his chest. So, he took the coward's way out and nodded his head, then walked out, shutting the door quietly behind him.

Once he reached his room, he shut the door and leaned against it, his head resting on the wood as his eyes closed. What he wanted to do was bang his head against it. He didn't deserve her thanks. He'd been a screw-up back then. Hell, he wasn't even sure that he still wasn't one right now. How could he have pulled a young girl away from her family, all because he'd seen something in her art and desired to exploit it? Sure, he'd cared for her safety. Sure, he'd cared enough to send Ethan to save her. But back then, that's all he'd done. Once she'd been delivered to his doorstep, he'd pretty much washed his hands of her.

Now she was back with stars in her eyes, and he felt like the lowest scum of the Earth. He walked over to his laptop and decided to do something right for once.

He was no Ethan Knight, but he knew his way around the internet and figured he could do some basic searching himself. To do any real digging, he'd need Ethan or his team to help out. He started with searching her family name and the town she was from. He didn't know why he remembered several details about her all of a sudden, but things started becoming clearer.

Her full name was Sannidhi Rangan. A simple search of that and Puri, India, brought up thirty-thousand possibilities. So he narrowed it down by adding her father's name, Haidar Rangan, which brought up just under twenty options.

He spent the next hour searching, researching until he felt he knew a little more about her family. One thing was clear to him now: they wouldn't stop until they got what they wanted. And from the looks of her family's affairs now, they wanted it all. They wanted her money, her freedom, her life. All for revenge.

Sandi had been engaged to Ishat Mahabir since the tender age of seven. Mitch's blood began to boil at this information. Seeing an engagement announcement in the local paper and the picture of the small seven-year-old Sandi standing next to a young man in his early twenties just pissed him off.

Apparently, Mahabir came from a wealthier family than Sandi's and when she disappeared the week before her wedding, her family was responsible. Basically, the Mahabir family ruined her family after she'd left. Almost all her family's power had been lost when Sandi had fled the country.

CHAPTER 4

The next morning, Sandi walked out of the bedroom after dressing and making sure the bed was made. When she opened the bedroom door, the place was quiet. She didn't think that Mitchell was there but to make sure, she walked across the landing and knocked on his door. When she was met with silence, she quietly opened his bedroom door. His bed was neat, almost as if he hadn't slept in it. His computer screen sat open and was set to a screen saver. She didn't mean to snoop, but an image of Mitchell and a tall brunette popped onto the screen. She took a few steps into the room and noticed how happy Mitch had looked. Looking at the brunette, she realized that it must be Suzanne. A smile was pasted on the woman's face, but her happiness didn't reach her eyes. Then the photo changed to one of Mitch and a taller, dark-haired man. Their arms were slung around each other and both had matching grins. She couldn't help it, she smiled at the image the pair made. She thought the picture had been taken at a sports game of some sort. She wasn't sure, but it looked like they were standing at a stadium.

When the photo switched again, she blinked and looked around his room. She could easily get caught up and watch his computer screen all day. Looking around the room, she noticed the design lines and color usage he used here. It was the same as in the rest of his place, simple with a hint of masculinity. There were several small touches here and there that reminded her a woman had once lived here. But for the most part, the space was all his.

She walked back out of his room and closed the door. Looking over the railing at the living room and kitchen below, she noticed again how silent it was. Taking the twisted staircase, she saw the note on the small stand at the bottom of the stairs. His phone sat in the charger next to a small bowl that held a set of keys and some loose change. Walking closer, she read his scratchy handwriting.

Sandi, I've gone out for a while. Help yourself to anything in the kitchen and make yourself at home. DON'T LEAVE THE APARTMENT FOR ANY REASON! I'll be back around one. -M

She smiled and took the note with her into the kitchen. She checked his kitchen and was pleased to see it was well stocked. Taking a large bowl down, she decided to make an old favorite of hers. Masala Dosa was a dish she hadn't made since she had been living at home. Taking a potato, onion, mushrooms, green peppers, and some of his seasonings, she got to work chopping and grilling in a large pan.

When the smells started mixing together, a memory of her mother flashed into her head. Sandi was young, around five. She was standing on a small stool in their large kitchen, her mother's hand holding hers as she helped her stir the contents in a large, flat pan. The smell and feel of her mother comforted her. Blinking, she realized that she hadn't thought of her mother in years, except in her dreams. She was shocked when a teardrop landed on her hand. Quickly wiping it away, she tried to focus on not burning her breakfast.

Two hours later, she was bored out of her mind. She'd cleaned his kitchen and the only evidence of her meal was a Tupperware container of leftover dosas in the refrigerator.

She'd tried to watch television, but her mind just wouldn't allow her to relax into any of the daytime shows. She'd walked into his large office on the main floor to look for a pad of drawing paper and found an old sketch pad. She found a few colored pencils and sat at his desk and tried to draw for a while. Again, her mind just wouldn't let her relax. She ended up walking around his office and weight room, looking at everything—his pictures, his books, even some of his paperwork. He had a small stack of bills on the end of his desk. She smiled when she realized he used the same internet service provider that she used.

She thought briefly about logging in to her account and transferring money into another more secure account, but she didn't know how her family had found her. Maybe they already had access to all of her money? Then she thought about emailing Eve. Again, questions were raised in her mind. She left his work laptop alone and decided she was better off waiting and discussing these things with Mitch when he got back.

She looked at the clock on the wall and realized she had two more hours before he was supposed to be back. Walking back into his gym, she saw the treadmill and decided some exercise would do her good. She went back upstairs and changed back into the shorts and found a smaller shirt. She looked in every closet for a pair of tennis shoes that would fit her. Finding nothing, she decided a pair of socks would have to work.

It took her a while to figure out the settings on the machine, but once she got it going, she settled into a relaxed pace. He had a flat-screen TV mounted on the wall above the machine. She had put on the news channel and was enjoying watching television as she worked out.

***

WHEN MITCH WALKED into his place almost an hour earlier then he'd expected, the rich aroma of spicy food hit him. He looked around for Sandi and the last thing he expected to see was her working out on his treadmill. He stood leaning against the wall, watching her tight backside in the skin-tight, black yoga shorts. He noticed she was only wearing socks and he felt a little guilty for not thinking about getting her some new clothing while he was out.

She was so engrossed in the news; she hadn't heard him come in. He was shocked when she stopped dead in her tracks on the treadmill. Of course, the force of the machine catapulted her backward, and she ended up landing on her butt a few feet away. He rushed to her side.

"Are you okay?" He knelt down beside her and noticed her face had gone very pale. Her eyes were glued to the television, so he looked to see what had caught her attention.

There was an older woman standing in a doorway, wearing a long housecoat. Her hair was up in curlers, and she was talking about Sandi.

"I hope she's okay. I just can't imagine who would do such a thing. This building was always so safe."

The television set showed a picture of an apartment, or what was left of one. A chair and table were in pieces. Then the image showed a picture of a mattress that had been slit open, as had the couch in the next picture. Painting supplies were thrown everywhere, broken into pieces. The dark paint was splattered on every surface.

"What do you think happened to your neighbor?" The reporter asked.

"I don't know. I haven't seen her since early yesterday. That poor dear." The older woman looked around frantically.

"What did the police say happened?" The reporter asked.

"Well, they think someone has taken her. They say there's enough evidence that they went ahead and filed a missing person report on her."

The reporter turned to the camera. "Samantha Rain is twenty-two, five-foot-four, one-hundred-five pounds." An image of Sandi flashed on the screen; it was a photo taken from her passport. "If anyone has seen this woman or has information on her whereabouts, please contact..."

Mitchell tuned out the rest. "Sandi?" He put his finger under her chin until she turned her head and looked at him. "We need to talk."

"Did you see the look on her face? She looked so... lost. I didn't know she cared that much. She's agoraphobic. What's this going to do to her?" He reached under her arms and pulled her up off the floor. Her eyes were still glued to the television set, staring as if she wasn't seeing the new report displaying. He turned her towards him, keeping his hands on her shoulders and pulling her into a light hug. The top of her head rested under his chin and he felt her tense her entire body.

"Sandi, she'll be okay. I'm sorry about your apartment. All your supplies and paintings." He felt her starting to relax.

"All that stuff doesn't matter to me. They're just supplies, they can be replaced. The paintings can be redone. But Mrs. Bernstein, she's older and very frail. I'm concerned about her. Maybe I should contact her. Let her know that I'm okay?" Sandi looked back towards the television.

"Sandi let's go in the living room and talk." He suggested.

She blinked a few times and looked at him. He could see

the tears forming in her dark eyes and wanted to gather her up again. She'd been through so much to get where she was, and now she was having to go through it again.

When he was sitting across from her in the living room, he could tell her mind was still focused on her neighbor and the news report.

"Sandi, I think we might have a bigger problem than dealing with your neighbor and the police. I'm not sure your paperwork from when you came into the US is legal." He said.

"What are you talking about?" She asked.

"I still can't get in touch with Ethan, and I'm a little worried that the channels he used to bring you into the States weren't completely legal." He leaned forward.

She thought about it, tilting her head slightly to the side. "I was sworn in as a citizen with special asylum. I'm a full-fledged American."

He thought about it and crossed off a couple other questions he'd been toiling over since her arrival. "That's good. Okay, that makes a few things easier."

"What are we going to do about the police? About them thinking I'm missing."

"I'll have to think about that. I want to make sure we look at every possible angle before we expose you to anything. Your father has some powerful connections; even here in the US."

"Alright. Then what's our next step?"

He got up and started to pace back and forth in front of the couch as she sat looking up at him. She was wearing an old pair of Suzanne's yoga shorts and one of his older tank tops. He couldn't help but notice how sexy she looked. She had used a large red rubber band to hold back her long hair so that her neck was exposed. He found the sight of her sitting cross legged on his coach in such comfortable wear very appealing.

"What?" she asked him, and he realized he'd been staring down at her.

He shook his head clear. "I'm sorry, I should have thought to grab you some more clothes while I was out. Next time I leave, I'll stop and get you whatever you need. Just make me a list."

"I don't mind going with you."

He shook his head. "Until we know more, I don't want you stepping foot outside this apartment. No phone calls either. I've already talked to my doorman who was on duty last night. He's sworn to secrecy. Now, with the news report, he may want to come to check on you to make sure I'm not the one holding you against your will."

She smiled and chuckled a little, and he realized what a wonderful sound it was. Her eyes lit up and he could tell for the first time she had forgotten her troubles for a minute. He would have done anything to see that look on her face again.

"I'd be happy to talk to him. He was very nice to me last night. His name was John, right?"

He nodded, impressed that she'd remembered. What he hadn't told her is that he'd also convinced John that she was in danger. He and the other doorman had agreed to watch out for her family. He'd shown the two men pictures of her father and cousin, which he'd printed from an old article online. Even though it was several years old, it was still a very clear shot of their faces.

He knew there were several things he still needed to accomplish today. First and foremost was explaining why he was going to be taking a few days off down at the office. He had a few meetings he knew he had to reschedule. Nothing major, just things he had to smooth over. He had a trip south next week that he'd have to reschedule as well.

"I've got a few more errands I need to run today. Why don't you make up that list so I can get you what you need? I'll be back later tonight."

She wrote up her list and he left thirty minutes later. On his way out, he talked to John and told him to swing by and check up on Sandi, so he knew she was perfectly safe. John had smiled.

"Mr. Kovich, you've lived in this building for over ten years. I know you would never kidnap that young woman. Besides, she walked into this building on her own, asking after you. I doubt a young woman like that would come looking for you if she didn't already know the kind of man you were."

He thought about John's words as he made his way out the door. He was right. Sandi must have known he would have helped her, otherwise, she would have never hunted him down.

During the short taxi ride to his office building, his mind tried to shuffle around his schedule. When he finally walked into the business he shared with Carter, he thought he had a plan and excuses he'd make to his secretary and staff.

Three hours later, he walked into a small boutique full of women's clothing with Sandi's list in hand.

She'd written in a very delicate handwriting only four items.

Tennis shoes – size seven
Pair of jeans – size three
Shirts – small
Sketchpad

He smiled at the last. Well, he could probably do better than just getting her a sketch pad. There was an art supply store, three buildings down. He'd make sure to get her everything she'd need to make sure her time stuck at his place would be bearable.

The first section he went to was the shoe aisle. He knew the kind of items he'd buy for himself but had no clue what a woman would buy for herself. He'd never done any practical shopping for Suzanne. For that matter, he realized, he'd never even shopped with her for clothing. He stood in the aisle and looked at over four dozen different kinds of tennis shoes.

Did she want running shoes? Walking shoes? There were so many kinds of women's shoes, he thought, the simple task of finding the right size was no longer the biggest issues.

"Can I help you?" Mitch turned to see a young woman with bright blue hair standing two feet away. The name tag on her shirt said, Starla.

"Yes, please. I'm looking for some shoes for my... girlfriend." He saw Starla's smile on her face and he felt a need to explain. "Her apartment was broken into and everything was stolen."

"Oh, I'm sorry to hear that. What kind of shoes are you looking for?" She sounded sympathetic.

"Tennis shoes, I think. Oh, and she'll need some other clothes." In for a penny, in for a pound, he thought. He might as well have this young girl help him pick out all of Sandi's clothing.

Half an hour and two hundred dollars later, he walked down the street and entered the art supply store weighted down with bags of items. At least here, he thought, he could easily figure out what she would need. After all, how hard could it be? It was just paper and pencils, right?

An hour and several hundred dollars later, he walked out of the store with two of the art store's employees following him. Everyone had their arms full of boxes and bags. The two boys helped him load everything into a waiting taxi and he made the short trip back home. Looking at his watch, he realized it was past seven. He'd hoped to be home before six.

His feet and back hurt from all the shopping, and he doubted he'd have the energy to cook tonight.

John helped him unload the bags and boxes, and between the two of them, they managed to make it up the elevator with his packages.

When he opened his door, he was greeted with the most wonderful smells.

CHAPTER 5

The six hours Sandi spent waiting for Mitch to come back were the longest in her life. Being limited on the things she could do had reminded her a lot of being back home. She was antsy and realized she was almost having a panic attack before she decided to get back on the treadmill.

At least when she was walking, she felt like she wasn't completely trapped. She desperately wished for her paints. She didn't know how Mrs. Bernstein could live trapped in the same rooms her entire life. Maybe Sandi had issues with not being able to leave a place because she'd been trapped in her house for most of her life. Since she was seven-years-old, she'd been limited in her movements. After all, her family had to protect and guide her, preparing her for her future.

But in the five years she'd lived on her own, she'd always enjoyed and marveled at her freedom to come and go. The first few months she had been on her own, she had found any reason not to be at home. She had spent hours out wandering the street markets near her apartment. She would spend hours at the library or at coffee shops or at the parks painting. She had even taken a day trip, riding the ferry across the water to visit the Statue of Liberty. It had been the most wonderful day.

After walking on the machine for over an hour, she went up and took a shower and got dressed in her own clothes again. She tried watching television, but when she'd seen her picture on the news again, she'd flipped off the set. Finally, she decided to make dinner, to do something nice for Mitch. She hadn't baked in a long time and always enjoyed making sweets when she'd been at home.

She'd been taught how to cook and bake from some of the finest chefs and bakers in India. Why not do something nice to show Mitch her appreciation?

She decided to make a full home-style meal. Everything from chole masala, a corn and tomato dish that happened to be one of her favorites, to khoya, a rich dessert. She enjoyed making the samosas, small pie-crust triangles filled with potatoes, peas, and seasons. Then she took her time making some potato pancakes stuffed with spicy seasoned meat, a dish her mother had taught her to make to perfection. The small round disks were perfect, and she enjoyed setting them on one of his larger burnt orange plates. The colors of her meals were as important to her as the taste. As an artist, she'd always found the color and texture of the food from her home as beautiful as any painting.

She got to work making prawn patties with curried cauliflower and chickpeas and set it all on a bed of white rice. She had found some green flat bowls and used those for each setting.

She followed up the patties with a tamarind fish curry. She placed the soup-like orange mixture in a dark brown square bowl she found in the back of one of his cupboards. She found some frozen salmon in his freezer and made curried salmon cakes with chopped onions and peppers to add the right mix of flavor and color.

To finish the meal off, she made khoya. Knowing it would keep her at the stove for over an hour only made it more appealing. She enjoyed matching each dish to a colored plate, and by the time she had the meal laid out, she felt like she'd used all her artistic abilities to make not only a delicious meal but a beautiful one. She topped the table off by lighting the tier candles and turning the lights lower. Then she waited nervously for him to arrive. The table was set with a meal fit for a king, and enough food to feed the entire building floor.

John followed Mitch in the door and Sandi instantly felt shy and embarrassed.

"Wow, it sure does smell good in here," John said, setting down the packages just inside the doorway.

Mitchell looked shocked. He stood in the doorway looking at the table and she wondered if she'd made the wrong choice of cooking so much.

"You…?" He cleared his throat, "You cooked all this?" He dropped the packages and walked to the table and looked at her. She nodded and looked down at her hands.

"It looks and smells wonderful." He turned back and nodded to John as the older man excused himself.

She stood there, looking at her hands. He walked over and put his finger under her chin until she looked at him.

"Sandi, you didn't have to cook all this. But I'm not going to turn any of it away. Not only does it smell delicious, it looks beautiful. I'm starving after all the shopping I've just done, so I might just eat every last drop myself." He chuckled.

She smiled at him, then nodded to all the boxes and packages he'd carried in. "What's all that?"

"Oh!" he clapped his hands and rubbed them together. "That, my dear, is your reward for working your fingers to the bone making all this food. But," he held up his finger when she started walking towards the packages, "not until after I've eaten. I did say I was starving." He smiled.

He wasn't joking about eating a lot. When they had sat down, she was amazed at how quickly he cleared several plates. He talked about his work as they ate, and she told him about her artwork and how she missed painting. Even though it had only been a day since she'd painted, to her it felt like weeks.

To which he stood and smiled at her, holding his hand out. "Dessert can wait."

She put her hand in his and he pulled her up and walked her over to the couch. "Sit." She sat and almost laughed at him as he tried to drag several packages over to her. "Don't open anything until I say so."

She couldn't help but notice that he was acting like buying things for her had given him pleasure, as well. She sat there waiting until the last package was piled around her. She was surrounded now. Large boxes sat on the floor, bags of every size crowded around her.

"You bought all this for me? I just wanted four things." She looked at it all.

"I know, but I've never gone shopping for a woman before, so I decided to over-do it." He sat in the chair across from her and put his chin in his hands as he leaned his elbows on his knees. "Plus, everything you had was pretty much destroyed in your apartment. This is just a small start to everything you needed to replace."

"Small?" She gestured to the large pile of bags and boxes.

"You can say the same about your dinner." He smiled as she laughed.

"True, I guess I did get carried away. I suppose I could forgive you for doing the same." She laughed again.

"Well..." He motioned to the bags.

She dug in. It was the first time anyone had ever bought anything for her, especially a man she wasn't related to. She could only remember her father giving her one gift her entire life. It was the night before her engagement. The small gold chain was a family heirloom; one she'd left behind.

Now as she opened a bag full of socks of every color and style, she wondered what he'd been thinking. "There must be over two dozen socks here."

"Yeah, well, they were having a sale." He smiled and grabbed a bag from the top of the pile. "Here, open this one."

She took the bag and smiled when she opened it and found a couple pairs of jeans her size. The next bag had shirts of bright colors. Did he know she enjoyed color? He must have because the more she opened, the more she realized he had picked out items she would have purchased herself. Shirts, skirts, pants, even the shoes were all items she would have picked out.

When she reached for a box next, he stopped her. "Wait, open the boxes last." She looked at him and she could see the eagerness in his eyes. She picked up another bag and found an elegant skirt of purple silk with a matching top.

"There are dress shoes," he searched the remaining bags and set a bag next to her. "here."

She slowly opened the bag and found an elegant pair of heels.

"For when you're free of this prison. I thought you'd enjoy going out." His kindness was overwhelming, she blinked back a tear. Not only had this man bought more clothes than she'd need in a year, he'd even thought to buy her a dress and heels. Something not practical, but something she'd enjoy wearing.

There was a bag of makeup and toiletries she hadn't thought to ask for.

"Yeah, well, I had some help picking out some items." He

said quietly when she set the bag aside. "Now, open the big box first." He smiled again.

She had to kneel down to get to the box. He sat on the floor next to her and helped her open it. When the lid was finally removed, she stopped in shock. In the box was her easel. Well, it couldn't have been hers, she'd seen her easel shattered in pieces on the news report as they panned around her studio.

She pulled out one of the pieces and enjoyed the smooth feel of the wood.

"I can put it together tonight." He said.

"Mitchell?" She was looking at the dark wood and when a tear slipped from her cheek, he leaned over and wiped it away. "You didn't have to do any of this for me."

"I know." He smiled.

She looked at him. His knees were touching hers as her legs were crossed, her long skirt tucked around her legs. She loved looking into his green eyes. His dusty blond hair had a slight curl to it and begged for her to run her fingers through it. He was so close, she could see small freckles on his nose and cheeks. Angel kisses. She'd always wanted angel kisses. She made the mistake of looking at his mouth and was transfixed by it. He had a slight dimple near the corner of his mouth on the right side.

"Sandi?" Her eyes traveled back to his eyes, just before he leaned over and took her mouth with his. It was her first kiss, and she was shocked at the smoothness of his lips. He smelled of spices, and when she opened her mouth, he dipped his tongue in and she tasted them and him. Her fingers were wrapped around the wood piece to her new easel, her fingers digging into the wood as his hand came up and gently ran up her neck to cup her hair and face. He tilted her head slightly and she dropped the piece of wood and gripped his shoulders. Even though she was sitting, she felt her world tilt when his mouth angled over hers, and he took her deeper then she'd ever been before.

She closed her eyes on a moan and felt her body starting to shake as his fingers gripped her hair, holding her gently to him. She never imagined it would feel like this, being this close to a man she had feelings for. She'd never denied how she felt towards Mitchell. At least not in her mind. He was her hero. The man who'd risked it all to save her. Sure, Ethan Knight had actually stuck his neck out physically, and she didn't discount what he'd done for her. But Mitchell had crossed that line, the one that most people wouldn't have, and he'd done it all to save her.

Ever since meeting him five years ago, she'd dreamed about him, about this. She slowly moved her fingers up his shoulders and ran them up his neck until they were where she wanted them to be, deep in his soft hair, holding him to her mouth as he continued to kiss her, causing small goose bumps all over her body.

Then he was pulling back and when she opened her eyes he was smiling at her. "I'm sorry, I didn't mean to go too fast. I can't believe how good you taste; how good you feel." He leaned his forehead on hers and she closed her eyes, trying to hold onto this moment forever. Then he pulled back and scooted back, handing her another package. "Here, there's more where that one came from."

AN HOUR LATER, Mitch had cleared a large space in his office. He'd put Sandi's new easel together and had carried every box into the room for her. She had disappeared upstairs to put her clothes away and when she came back down, she was wearing a pair of her new jeans and one of her new shirts. He smiled and couldn't help feeling proud that he'd picked items that not only looked very good on her but looked her style. It was hard to explain, she just looked right wearing the clothes he'd bought for her.

"They look great on you." She walked over looking a little shy, her cheeks turning a soft color of pink. He didn't know where that kiss had come from earlier, but he'd been sitting there admiring her and the next minute he'd been devouring her.

He really needed to control himself. He could tell she was inexperienced, and he didn't want to scare her or go too fast. He was supposed to be protecting her, not sleeping with her.

She picked up a large canvas and a box with the tubes of oil paints and various brushes the clerk had suggested.

"I can't wait to get back to it."

"Now?" He looked around. It was a quarter to ten and he doubted he'd be able to stay up much longer. After all, he didn't even get any sleep last night. He'd spent the entire night on his laptop searching for a way to get her out of the mess he'd gotten her into.

"You don't have to stay and watch." She started setting the paints down on the small table he'd set near the easel for her. "I have a strong urge to paint that I've been avoiding for a full day now." She turned to him. "You look tired. I bet you didn't even sleep last night."

He nodded and realized he was exhausted. "If you need anything..."

"I won't. When I start painting, I pretty much ignore everything else around me." She turned around to start working.

"Okay, well..." He started backing up. "Enjoy. Goodnight." When he realized she was focused on the task of organizing her paints, he smiled at her back and then turned and left.

Taking the stairs slowly, he walked into his room and decided a shower might help clear his head of her. But before he walked into the bathroom, he checked his messages. He still hadn't heard from Ethan. Deciding to try one more time, he picked up the phone. On the third ring, it went to Ethan's voice-mail and he left another message for his friend.

He didn't know what else to do except to hide her until Ethan could enlighten him as to how he could hide a full grown human being in a city of over eight million.

The next morning when he walked into his office he was shocked to see her still at it. She'd laid one of his old sheets on the floor underneath the easel and he could see paint splattered on it from across the room.

"Good morning." She jumped and turned to look at him when he walked in carrying a coffee cup.

"Is it morning already?" She smiled and when he walked closer to her, she reached out and took his mug and drank some of his coffee. "Mmmm, my favorite."

Damn, he thought, he'd worked it out in his mind last night to not be attracted to her. It was all very logical in his thoughts. He'd told himself it was only natural that he'd found her attractive. After all, it had been almost half a year since he'd been with anyone, physically.

But when she licked her lips and took another sip of his coffee, he knew it was more than just attraction. He was in full-blown lust. Taking the coffee mug from her, he set it down on the small table and took a step closer to her. Her eyes were focused; her hair was pushed up in a clip he'd purchased at the clerk's suggestion. Slowly reaching up, he let her hair down and played with a red streak that ran the entire length.

"I like this." He smiled when he noticed her eyes cloud over. She stood with her paintbrush in one hand, down by her side, forgotten as he took one more step towards her, blocking out any space between them. He knew what he was doing, he was following his instinct as he leaned down and took her mouth.

The sweet coffee was on her tongue; her lips were softer than he remembered last night. She was softer. She was short, and he wrapped his arms around her waist as he leaned over to take the kiss deeper. Then she was wrapping her arms around him and pushing herself up onto her toes as he moaned and tried to stay in control of himself.

He couldn't remember it being like this with anyone else. He didn't think he could take much more of this without carrying her up the stairs, so he pulled back and tried for a casual smile. How could he have known that he would be shaken to the core over a simple morning kiss?

"Good morning."

She laughed when he said this again. "Yes, it is now."

He enjoyed her smile. Her entire face lit up and her eyes sparkled.

"Can I see your progress or are you one of those moody artists that don't want anyone to see a painting until it's completed?"

She shook her head, "No, I'm not moody, please." She motioned for him to look at the canvas and stood back so he could stand in front of the easel.

He'd never seen anything like it. The colors alone drew the eye. Then he stepped closer and he could see the small circles, each one delicately placed so as a whole, they made an image that almost shocked him. He'd seen paintings of landscape before, but none as detailed and all of it made from those small circles. He wondered if her wrist and hands hurt after a full night of drawing circles. Turning, he smiled as he noticed her rubbing her hands and wrists.

"This is incredible. I can't even begin to imagine how you do something like this."

"Patience." She smiled and walked over and stood next to him. "I'm not quite finished, but I think I'll take a break and grab something to eat and maybe steal some more of your coffee."

She smiled up at him and he knew he was in more trouble than he had previously thought.

After fixing them some scrambled eggs, he told her he had a few things he had to do today and left for his meetings before he'd be free for the next few weeks. He didn't like lying to her, but he didn't want her to know that he planned on going to her apartment building to see if her father and cousin were still hanging around.

He was no Ethan Knight, but he thought the simple task of staking out a building couldn't be that hard. As he rode in the taxi the fifty blocks downtown, he thought about the kisses. Why was it that when he wasn't around her, he could think rationally that it was a bad idea to kiss her? But when he was with her, all he thought about doing was kissing her again.

He asked the taxi driver to drop him off a few blocks away. As he started walking towards her building, his eyes and mind were focused on looking for her father and cousin. He would have missed the dark sedan parked a block away by the pier if she hadn't mentioned seeing it that first night. He casually walked to the pier and leaned against the railing, looking out at the river. To anyone else, he was just a man taking in the sunny day. Behind his sunglasses, however, he watched the sedan. Its windows were tinted, and he was wondering how he'd get a better look to see if the outline of a man sitting in the driver's seat was indeed one of Sandi's relatives.

He must have stood there, leaning against the railing, for fifteen minutes before he got a break. The window of the sedan slid down slowly, and someone threw a cigarette butt out. Sandi's cousin Anish sat in the driver's seat, watching the people come and go in front of her building.

He wondered where her father was as he started walking to find a taxi. Then he stopped in the middle of the sidewalk, shocked as he spotted Sandi just across the street. She was walking quickly and right towards the black sedan.

By the time he'd crossed the street and was half a block away from them, she was already fighting her cousin off with impressive moves. He started running just as he heard her scream. Then she took off running in the opposite direction with her cousin right on her heels.

CHAPTER 6

Sandi was back at her easel working with the television on, when another report came through. This time Mrs. Bernstein was standing outside her building, looking frail and lost. She was again begging for whoever had Sandi to return her, safe and sound.

Dropping her paintbrush, she ran to the door and out it, only one thing on her mind: calling Mrs. Bernstein. She'd passed by dozens of pay phones on the way there. She didn't know if any of them worked still, but she was willing to take a chance since she didn't want to call from Mitchell's phone, just in case they could track it back to him. She just wanted to tell her friend that she was okay. That she was alive and not in any danger.

When she entered the lobby, she saw John standing outside, just in front of the doors. His back was to her, and she quickly and quietly moved behind a large plant so that if he turned, he wouldn't be able to see her. She didn't think he'd let her just walk out, not after talking with Mitchell and knowing what she was going through. So, she had to figure out how to get out of the building without John knowing.

Looking around, she noticed a side hallway and saw daylight coming from it. Moving towards the light, she turned a corner and saw that someone had propped the fire exit open with a brick. Rushing out the door, she made it a few blocks away before she started looking for a payphone. When she found one, she knew her neighbor's number by heart and quickly dialed it.

"Hello?" Her voice was a little strained.

"Mrs. Bernstein, it's me San... Samantha. I'm okay. I'm not hurt. I'm..." She broke off as a deeper voice broke on the line.

"Sannidhi?" The accent was thick, and her heart stopped, and her vision grayed. Hearing her cousin's voice on the other end of the line scared her. What was he doing with Mrs. Bernstein?

"Sannidhi?" He repeated.

"Yes, Anish. I'm here." She whispered.

Thirty minutes later, she approached the dark sedan with a plan. She would do whatever she needed to ensure that Mrs. Bernstein was safe.

When she got closer to the car, she noticed only one person in the car. What had he done with Mrs. Bernstein? Where was her father?

Her cousin stepped from the car and tried to grab her arm. Sandi knew she needed to stay in sight of people. There was no way she was going to get in the car with her cousin.

"What do you want Anish?" She asked, keeping her shoulders straight.

"For you to pay. Come with me." He reached for her again.

"No!" She jerked back. "What have you done with Mrs. Bernstein?"

"The old lady wouldn't leave her apartment. When I tried to pull her with me, she fainted. I didn't want to carry her, so I left her there on her floor." He reached for her again, grabbing her arm in a tight grip. She spun and did one of the moves she'd been taught the first few months of self-defense classes. When he reached for her again, she twisted away, this time stomping on his foot really hard with the heel of her new shoes. He grabbed her around the waist, so she started screaming like she'd been taught to do. He released her when everyone within a block radius looked in their direction. When she was free, she took off running to the one place she knew she would be able to lose him. The street market was only three blocks away. It was always crowded, and she knew she could easily lose him in the crowds.

She heard him yelling for her and could tell how close he was behind her. She was a fast runner, had always been faster than her cousin, but she was working on little sleep. When she heard him getting closer and closer, she panicked. People looked at her as she ran past them, some moved out of her way, others didn't. When she rounded the final corner and the street market was finally in sight, she felt her cousin's hand grip her shirt. He jolted her shoulder back as he grabbed it. She heard a rip and then she was able to jerk her shoulder free.

Freed, she decided to take a risky chance and darted into the street. She made it halfway across the busy intersection before she heard tires screech and a horn blast, right before she felt the impact of the taxi on her hip.

MITCH WAS RIGHT on Sandi's cousins' heels, but when he rounded the corner, he saw Sandi bolt across the street. He began to scream her name just before the taxi clipped her hip. He watched in horror as her body gained air and flew across the street, landing in a small pile a few feet away from him.

People stopped at the noise, some began to run towards her from the street market. He watched her cousin stop on the sidewalk, look around at the people, then casually walk away. Mitch rushed to Sandi's side, pushing several people away as they stood around her to stare.

There was no blood, he thought as he knelt beside her. He knew better than to move her, so he gently touched her face. "Sandi?" he said over and over, lightly rubbing his fingers over her face. When she moaned and turned her head, he held her still. "No, don't move." He looked up to a woman standing across from him. "Call an ambulance."

"Already on it," she said, shaking her phone.

He gently ran his hands over Sandi, checking for broken bones. When he got to her hip, she woke quickly and bolted up letting out a little scream, then she started to fight him off.

"Easy, you're okay. It's me." He said, and she stopped, looking up at him. In the next moment, she was in his arms and everyone around them began to clap and cheer.

Over an hour later, they were still stuck in the small room in the ER, waiting for a doctor to tell her what he already knew: no broken bones, just some bad bruising. But the doctor had wanted an X-ray and so they were waiting for her turn to be rolled into the x-ray room. She was a trooper through it all. They had given her a mild pain pill. She had a slight bump to the back of her head where she'd landed on the cement, but he didn't see a scratch on her. He was thankful.

The police had come and gone. They both explained everything several times to several different officers. The missing person's report was updated and when they finally left the small hospital room, he believed the police were going to look for her family for questioning. He got the impression that they didn't mark it as a high priority.

Mitch had held back his temper at her for leaving his place since she'd explained everything several times. He sat across from her in a very uncomfortable chair, watching her closely. How did she learn to kick butt like that?

"Why are you looking at me like that?" She asked.

He uncrossed his arms and tried to relax. "Like what?"

She looked at him more closely. She was propped up in one of the beds with several pillows behind her head. Her new jeans were ripped at the knee and her shirt was a complete loss. He'd given her the light jacket he'd been wearing to cover herself.

"I don't know like you're trying to figure me out. Mitch, I've already explained why I went to meet my cousin." She looked tired.

"I know." He said, starting to feel bad.

"I'm just thankful Mrs. Bernstein is okay. If anything had happened to her..." She started.

"Don't." He broke in, stopping her from the deep thoughts. "Don't do that to yourself. You heard what the cops said. She's fine and going to stay with her son for a while. She was just happy to hear that you were okay."

"I know. It's sad. I didn't even know that much about her. I had lived there three years and talked to her almost every day, but I didn't know she had a son." She closed her eyes for a few seconds. He could see her frowning and got up to cross the room. Taking her hand, he waited until she looked at him.

"Sandi, I've lived in my building for over ten years. The only people I talk to on a regular basis are John and Matt, the two doormen. Neighbors have come and gone. I'm courteous to them, but short of saying a few words in the elevator, I don't know much about them." She looked down at their joined hands.

"You risked too much for someone else. I'm trying to understand why you would do something like that."

"Mrs. Bernstein was the first person I knew outside of the people who helped me settle here. She was my first friend. She always cared about me. Where I was going, what I was doing. She's the sweetest person I've ever known. You would have done the same thing."

He looked down at her and could see tears forming in her eyes. "You're right. It doesn't mean I am condoning you doing something so risky. But I can understand."

Just then the nurse walked in with a wheelchair to take her to get her x-ray. He sat in the small room and thought about her. There really was more to her than even she thought. This was New York. People tended to stick to their own business here. No one really stood up for their neighbors that much, anymore. Yet here she was, bruised all because she had thought her little old neighbor lady was in danger.

Two hours later, they walked in the front door of his building. Matt was on duty tonight and he was shocked to see Sandi hobbling in the front door, leaning on Mitch for support. Thank goodness she hadn't broken any bones. She'd been very lucky. She was having a hard time walking and when they finally made it in the door, he swooped her up and carried her the rest of the way into his place and gently set her down on the couch. He could tell she was tired. Her eyes were dull and when he'd carried her, she had rested her head on his shoulder.

Then he remembered that she'd spent the entire night painting. She must be exhausted.

"I can carry you upstairs if you want?" He stood over her as she adjusted her legs on the couch. She shook her head, no.

"No, I think I'll stay down here for a while. What are your plans?" She asked him.

He thought about it. "Well, there's a game on tonight. I suppose if you're game, we could watch it down here. I could make us some sandwiches and popcorn?"

"That sounds wonderful." She adjusted her legs a little more. He realized she was trying to get comfortable and walked over to retrieve the pillows from one of the chairs. Propping it behind her, he handed her the blanket off the back of the couch. She was still wearing her torn jeans and his jacket, but still acted like she was cold. Could it be that she was still in shock? He didn't want to take any chances. He helped her lay the blanket over her gently.

"Thank you." She straightened the blanket over her lap. He turned to walk into the kitchen. "Mitch?" He turned back to her. "I mean it, thank you for everything you've done for me. I don't know what I would have done if you hadn't been here."

He smiled at her and nodded. "Here." He handed her the remote. "The game is on ESPN."

He walked into the kitchen and felt like banging his head on the wall. He didn't want her gratitude. Didn't she understand she was in this mess because of him? He walked to the fridge and started making them some turkey sandwiches.

By the time he walked back into the living room with his arms full of food, he stopped dead in the middle of the floor when he realized she was asleep. Her head was tilted back on the pillow, her arms were crossed over her chest lightly, and her face was more beautiful than he had remembered. He was really in trouble.

Setting the food down on the dining room table, he walked over and muted the game, then bent over and gathered her up in his arms and carried her upstairs to her room.

When he started to lay her on the bed she moaned and tried to keep her arms around his shoulders. "Mitch?"

"Shh, you're okay. I'm just putting you to bed." He murmured.

"Stay with me for a while? I don't want to be alone." She sighed when his head hit the soft pillow.

He looked into her sleepy eyes and nodded. After laying her down gently, he walked to the end of the bed and removed her shoes one by one. Then he toed off his own and crawled into the bed beside her. Making sure the blanket was firmly covering her, he pulled her into his arms. He relaxed as she sighed and snuggled closer.

"Thank you, Mitch." She said as he kissed the top of her head and wondered if there would ever be a time when her thanking him wouldn't sting so much.

CHAPTER 7

Sandi woke alone, sore, hungry, and in desperate need of a shower. She didn't know how long she had slept, but she did feel a little refreshed. When she moved to the end of the bed, her hip screamed with pain. Using the night table to help her stand, she tested her strength slowly. When she finally got fully upright, she realized the pain wasn't as bad as she had thought it would be. Three steps later, she realized she'd been wrong. When she walked, her hip joint felt like it was grinding. By the time she made it into the bathroom, her pain level had tripled.

"Okay, so I'll be staying off my feet for a while," she told her reflection, then she noticed that she looked a mess. She was still wearing Mitchell's jacket and when she removed it and hung it on the hook on the back of the door, she cringed at the shape her new shirt was in. The whole back seam was torn. Her new jeans were torn on each knee, as well.

Slowly removing each item, she tossed her shirt in the small waste bin. When she started to remove her jeans, she gasped at the large bruise running down her left side. She assumed that her hip had taken the brunt of the weight when she'd landed. When she finally pulled her jeans all the way off, she tossed them in the bin as well.

Turning to get a better look at her left side, she realized it wasn't just her front that was bruised. Her entire left butt cheek was purple. She'd never had a bruise so big before. After looking at it for a few minutes, she walked over and started to run a bath, thinking that it might be easier for her to sit rather than stand to clean up. She moved the shampoo and soaps down to the bottom shelf so she could easily reach them. Then she climbed into the hot water and almost cried with relief when the heat hit her hip.

She didn't know how long she stayed in the hot bath, but when she felt her head getting dull she finally climbed out. What she needed now was a clean set of clothes and a large cup of coffee.

A few minutes later, when she walked out onto the landing, Mitch walked out of his room.

"So, how are you feeling?" he asked as he approached her. She noticed he wasn't wearing a suit and wondered if he was going to go into work that day since it must be past nine already.

"A little sore. I have a large bruise across my hip." She said.

He frowned at that and she realized when he did so, a small crease formed between his eyebrows.

"We should have iced it last night. I bet you're hungry." He said.

She nodded her head. "I could use a quart of coffee at this point, too." He chuckled.

"Do you think you can maneuver the stairs yourself? Or do you want me to carry you again?" He asked.

She blushed, remembering how she had sighed and laid her head on his shoulder as he carried her upstairs last night. It had been the stuff of dreams, being held by his strong arms, her head resting against his chest. She desperately wanted it to happen again, but she was too afraid he'd realize her thoughts.

Shaking her head, she started walking towards the stairs, holding onto the wood railing tightly. By the time she made it to the bottom, she was breathing hard and a bead of sweat rolled down her forehead. He was beside her the entire trip down, his hands out just in case she started to topple.

"You're staying on that couch all day." He was frowning at her when she looked up, and she could see the worry in his eyes.

She nodded in agreement and started walking towards the living area. A few steps further and he scooped her up, carrying her the ten feet to the couch. When he set her down gently, she wished the room was larger so that he'd have to hold onto her longer.

"I'll get you that coffee and an ice pack." He turned and walked out of the room. Reaching over, she grabbed the remote and turned on the television and was shocked to see her face on the set again.

"*...apparently was involved in an altercation yesterday. Police aren't saying where the young woman is now, just that she is uninjured and under protection.*"

The end of the report was all she needed. She flipped off the set and tossed the remote down.

If her cousin or father asked enough questions, they would be able to find her connection to Mitchell and her safe haven would be exposed. She needed to move on. Her mind worked frantically as she heard Mitch making her coffee in the kitchen. She knew he wouldn't let her go on her own, so she started making plans on how she would sneak away and where she would go.

Maybe back at the shelter was the best place for her at this time? Regardless, she needed to make a choice on what she was going to do and act on it soon. She doubted she had a week before her cousin and father would find the connection.

"What are you scheming?" Mitch walked in balancing a tray holding a cup of coffee, a bowl of fruit, and some toast on a plate. He set the tray on the coffee table and sat across from her.

"What?" She tried to look innocent. Apparently, it wasn't working.

"You have something on your mind. You might as well spill it. I'm known for getting my way." The smile he gave her almost stopped her heart.

How could she hide anything from him? She tried to start talking about what had happened yesterday, but he stopped her.

"Sandi, I know there is something else on your mind. You get a small crease here." He reached up and touched her forehead. Almost the same place she'd noticed his earlier. "Don't tell me you're just thinking about what happened to Mrs. Bernstein. You know she's safe at her son's."

She closed her eyes and sighed. "I was thinking of leaving."

"Where do you think you could go that you'd be safer than here? Or is it just me you're trying to get away from?" He leaned forward, resting his arms on his knees.

Her eyes flew open. "No!" She was shocked that he would think that about her. "Of course not. It's just that you've done so much for me. You've helped me more than I could ever repay."

"Helped you?" He looked disgusted. "I've done nothing but put you in the direct path of danger, since the night I first talked to you. I wish I would have never gotten involved. You'd be better off, living a life without all this fear."

She stood up, shocked. "How can you say that? Do you even remember why I called you, begging for your help?"

He shrugged his shoulders and kept his eyes focused on her feet. "I just assumed it was to get out of an arranged marriage."

"You helped me escape mutilation at the hands of my fiancé's family. They were going to perform the mādā janānga vikrti."

Upon his blank look, she closed her eyes and blurted out. "Also known as female genital mutilation. My future husband's family wanted to make sure I was pure and that I would stay that way. They were concerned that my art was westernizing me, that I'd become too uncontrollable. My family could do nothing but bend to their wishes. Especially since they had paid bride's wages for me when I was only seven-years-old. Which my family squandered selfishly on large houses, fast cars, and god knows what else." She walked to the window, ignoring the pain in her hip, instead focusing on the pain in her heart. She looked out the window at the crowds of people, wishing she could disappear among them and never be seen or heard from again.

She jumped a little when his arms came around her, holding her back to his chest. His lips brushed her hair.

"I'm sorry. I didn't know." He pulled her until she turned and then he wrapped his arms around her. She did the same, holding onto him, and for the first time in her life, she felt completely safe and knew that no matter what happened, he would protect her.

She pulled back and looked into his face. Taking a chance at what she wanted, she pulled his head down to meet hers in a light kiss that would show him how much she appreciated everything he'd done. How much she cared about him. His hands felt wonderful as they rubbed up and down her back and arms. She wondered what they would feel like on her bare skin, what he would feel like as she ran her fingers over his heated skin.

She'd seen him in just a towel the first night and wanted to see him like that again. She'd dreamed about it, about being with him. Pouring everything she had into the kiss, she leaned up and wrapped her hands in his hair.

His hands continued to run over her, causing small fires on her skin under her clothes. Then she felt him slowly lift her shirt and touch her skin, just near her waist. On a moan, she leaned into his hands as his mouth took her to a level she'd never known was possible.

"Please," she moaned against his mouth. "Mitch, please. Touch me."

He leaned back, hovering just a breath from her mouth, and looked into her eyes. His emerald eyes sparkled, and she could see his desire for her plainly. Pulling back a little, he shook his head. "Sandi, I don't think it would be fair. Here, sit. We need to talk."

He helped her back to the couch where she took a deep drink of the lukewarm coffee to help settle herself. When he sat across from her again, she felt a little part of her break.

"Don't look at me like that. Like I've just killed your puppy. Sandi, you don't know me." He held up his hand as she started to deny it. "You don't. You came in here the other night, and I hadn't thought about you once in five years. Back then..." He ran his hands through his hair, causing parts of it to stand up a little. "Back when you arrived in America, I wasn't myself. I wasn't the best person I could be. I didn't have my life in order. I drank a lot."

She looked down at his hands as he gripped them together. "I know."

"No, you don't. I was an alcoholic by twenty. I can't even begin to compare my family problems to yours, but let's just say my childhood wasn't all rainbows. So, when I was a teen,

I picked up a bottle, and I didn't put it down again until I almost killed a person that someone close to me cared about." He hung his head for a moment. She silently sat there, watching him, waiting. "Sandi," he looked back up at her. "You deserve someone...better."

"Mitch, I think I know what I deserve. Especially coming from what and where I have and going through everything I have. I knew what you were five years ago. I did stay here for a few nights, remember?" He shook his head, no. "Well, I was there to pick you up off the floor the second night I was here. I helped you back into bed. I knew you were in a bad spot. But underneath it all, I could see what kind of man you were, what you would become. Walking in here the other night only confirmed it. You took me in again, no questions. No demands. No thoughts to your own safety."

He looked at her for a while. She could tell he was trying to figure her out. Then he shook his head and smiled. "Eat your food. If you want more, I'll make something bigger. I have a few errands to run today, but I'll be back later." He stood, and she could tell the conversation was over.

"Would you bring me the new sketch pad, the box of chalk, and pens? I'm stuck on the couch for the day, but it doesn't mean I can't do something I enjoy." She smiled.

"Sure, is there anything else?" He asked.

She held up her cup. "More coffee?"

AN HOUR later Mitchell walked into Carter's office, interrupting a heated conversation between his partner and Eve, who was their top employee and best friend for longer than he knew. His two friends had recently seemed to never get along. Once, Mitchell had asked Carter if they should fire Eve, to which Carter replied, "Why on god's earth would I want to get rid of our best asset?" He'd followed it up with, "Don't you ever tell her I said that." Knowing it was just a little game the two friends played, he shut the door loudly and smiled as the pair jumped and glared at him.

"Hello, why don't you two just get a room and get it over with." He chuckled at the similar looks of horror the pair made at his suggestion.

"What do you want? I thought you were off for the next few weeks." Carter sat down behind his desk and waved him in, then he looked at Eve. "You can handle that client on your own."

Eve put her hands on her hips and stood there, glaring down at him. Finally, Carter sighed and said, "Fine, I'll make the call later."

She smiled and started to walk out of the room. "Mitchell, I hope you're enjoying your vacation."

He knew she didn't like him laughing at how well she could handle his friend, so he just nodded his head as she walked past him. But when the door was shut, he burst out laughing.

"Man, the least you can be doing is sleeping with her to end up that whipped." Mitch sat down.

Carter glared at him. "That woman knows more tricks to get what she wants than you and I put together."

They both chuckled at that. "Of course, it doesn't help that she looks like a Greek goddess." Mitch put in.

"Yeah, there is that." Carter smiled and looked at a stack of papers on his desk. "What are you doing here?"

"Well, I need your help." He said, leaning back in the chair.

"Shoot." His friend gave him his full attention.

"I need to take Sandi somewhere safe for a while, after she heals from the whole ordeal yesterday. Someplace not traceable to any of us." He'd thought about it, and Carter was his only outlet for ideas.

Carter leaned back in his chair and thought about it. "You still haven't heard from Ethan?"

Mitch shook his head, no. He hadn't kept any details from his friend and knew Carter would guard it with his life. After all, they'd been best friends growing up.

Carter was the complete opposite of Mitch in every way. His dark hair, eyes, and skin weren't the only things he was talking about, either. Carter was a businessman, always looking at the angles of every deal. Mitch tended to go with his gut and heart. It was hard to explain, but Mitch could just tell how a person was if they were going to be a good investment or be a flake and not worth the time.

The agency worked well with the pair of them. Mitchell's heart and Carter's business smarts had proved a lethal combination. Since starting the business, they'd built the company to what it was today; a company with over three thousand high-profile clients and growing.

"Hmmm, I might know someplace; my grandparents' place. I'll have to get back to you, make sure my neighbor has time to prepare it for you. When are you thinking of leaving?" Carter asked.

"Well, in a day or two, I suppose. She can barely walk right now." Mitch frowned.

His friend nodded, "I hope she's okay."

"Yes, just bruised." He thought about seeing Sandi trying to make it down the stairs and frowned a little more.

"Eve keeps asking about her. She feels so bad that she couldn't be there to help her." Carter said.

"I know, but I think the less attention we draw, the better. We still don't know how they found out about her. The only thing we can come up with is through K&E." Mitch sat forward now.

Carter frowned. "I'd hate to think that someone working for us would be the cause." He shook his head. "I doubt it. No one, not even Eve, knew Sandi's real name. It's not like it's in her file. Trust me, I've checked. Her cover wasn't blown by us."

Mitch released a sigh. He'd guessed as much, but hearing it come from his friend made him feel more confident.

"I'll check on this and get back to you later this week." Carter stood, and Mitch followed, then noticed a young blond woman standing in Carter's doorway. Lisa was Carter's latest catch. Even though she was ten years younger than Carter, it didn't seem to fizzle the relationship.

As Mitchell walked out, he realized Sandi was exactly ten years younger than him. Shaking his head, he stepped into the elevator and asked himself what he'd gotten himself into.

CHAPTER 8

When Mitch walked into his place a few hours later, Sandi was fast asleep on the couch. A ball game was blaring on the television set, but he doubted she'd been watching it. He walked over and switched off the set then looked at her sketch pad. Taking it with him, he walked into the kitchen as he flipped through the drawings.

There were some sketches of beautiful scenery, all very well detailed and extremely good. Then he stopped on one of himself, and he sat at the bar stool, just looking at it. He'd never seen a drawing of himself before. Is that really what he looked like? What did she think of him?

He must have studied the drawing for a while. When he looked up, Sandi was standing on the opposite side of the bar, watching him. He hadn't even heard her walk into the room.

"Well?" She sat at the bar stool on the other side, looking at him.

"It's incredible. I've never seen anything like it." He looked up at her again. "I didn't know you drew people."

"I normally don't, but I make exceptions for people who matter." She smiled.

There was something in her eyes. Something he couldn't deny himself. The attraction wasn't the problem. Hell, he was a man after all. Wanting an attractive woman was in his nature. But it was what was lying underneath that attraction that scared him.

He'd been burned before and the fact that he was finding it hard to trust women, especially sexy women, made him realize he had to think about taking it slow. Besides, he didn't know exactly what experience she had with men. He did know she wasn't that schooled. Oh, it wasn't as if she was a bad kisser. Hell, she'd lit him on fire with her naivety of it all. He'd never realized that he'd find the lack of experience in a woman so thrilling. Actually, it had made him want to see how much farther he could get with her. He thought about how naive she was and how much fun it would be to teach her, slowly.

"What?" Her question broke his trance.

"Hmm?" He tried to play his horny thoughts off.

"Mitchell, just like you told me before, there are some expressions you can just read on a person. You were just looking at me like you wanted to devour me." She smiled, shyly. "I don't mind it, you know."

He shook his head and set the sketchpad down. "I do. We need to keep our heads clear. We need to come up with a plan." He turned and started pulling food from the refrigerator. He was running low on supplies and would have to make a run to the local market soon.

"Mitch? I'm worried about my money." She said out of the blue.

He stopped and turned. "What do you mean?"

"Well, I haven't touched my accounts since seeing my

father and cousin. I'd like to ensure that it's all still there. If I can use your computer...?"

He thought about it and saw no possible way that her cousin or father could trace her bank account login to his machine. Not without one of them being the best hacker on the earth.

"Your father or cousin aren't computer geniuses, are they?" He asked.

She laughed, "No, my father didn't even know how to answer his cell phone for over two months. My cousin Anish knows a little about computers, but I don't think either of them would know how to trace your connection." She started to frown. "Now, my uncle, Adham..." he saw her shiver. "My father's brother knew the most about computers. But he's in a federal prison in Colorado."

"He's the one that tried to kill my friend Ric?" Mitch asked.

She nodded. "He always scared me. He looked at me...like I was property. I always made sure my father was in the room with me when he was around. At least after I hit the age of ten."

He looked at her and thought about wringing her family's necks, every single one of them.

"I take back what I said earlier." He tried for a casual tone but knew his voice sounded rough. "I'm glad I helped you escape those people. I'm glad you're here, safe."

She smiled at him and he felt something shift inside, something he'd never felt before. A barrier being lifted. How had she moved him to this so quickly? He didn't even know that much about her, and here he was falling hard and fast.

He pulled out the kitchen knife and cutting board. "So, while I whip us up dinner, how about you tell me all about Sandi?"

She smiled and leaned on the counter top and started

talking about her life up until the point where she'd banged on his door a few nights ago.

Later that night, when he couldn't sleep, he headed downstairs to use the equipment in his gym. He found that working out curbed his desire to have a drink. He knew it was part of his recovery, finding something to replace that feeling, and lifting had taken its place. He not only felt healthier for it but more centered in life. There was no way he'd ever fall off the wagon, as long as he could move his body.

LATER THAT NIGHT as Sandi lay in bed, she listened to a storm brewing outside. She watched the lightning streak across the empty room as she stared at the ceiling and thought of Mitch. Was he lying in his bed thinking of her?

She had no experience when it came to love or sex. She knew what she wanted, but not how to get it, and she didn't think she had the courage to take it herself. But after almost an hour of lying there watching the rain on the window, she pushed back the covers and walked out her door. If he was asleep, she'd turn around and crawl back in her bed, alone. If she looked in on him and he was awake...well, she didn't know what she'd do.

Standing outside his door, she reached for the doorknob. Then she heard his workout equipment clang from downstairs. Curious, she headed downstairs and was surprised that he was lifting weights at this time of night. She pushed the door wide and looked into the dim room. The TV was going with no sound and she watched with excitement as Mitch lifted a bar with heavy weights on it above his head. He was bare-chested, and she realized she could have stood there watching him for hours.

"Come here." She thought she heard a chuckle when she jumped.

"You should be asleep."

"So, should you. Come over here." He set the bar of weights down and sat up on the bench.

She cautiously moved into the room, and when she got about a foot away, he reached up and grabbed her. Before she knew it, she was sitting on his lap as she nervously laughed.

"Why are you still up at," he looked at the clock on the wall, "a quarter till one in the morning?"

"I... I couldn't sleep."

"You couldn't? And you thought I could do something about that?" He started running his hands over her soft tank top, his hands making small little circles on her stomach. She felt like purring. She realized her hands were pinned between them and when she moved to get them free, he shook his head.

"I know what you thought. It's right there on your face." He lifted her in one quick motion and started walking out of the room.

"Where?" She started to ask.

"I'll just help you get back to bed." He smiled down at her. She thought he meant to carry her back to her room but was shocked when he walked into his own door. He left the lights off and walked to the edge of the bed where he laid her down gently.

She started to ask him what he was doing.

"No, sssh. I'll help you." His hands moved downward until he reached the bottom of her shirt, then he slowly inched the soft material up, exposing her heated skin, pushing it higher until she was almost exposed to his view. She wanted to pull her shirt down and run back to her room. What had she been thinking? How could she have been this foolish to expose herself? Then he gently touched her, and all thoughts of escape fled her mind. How could she not want this?

Closing her eyes, she rolled her head back on a moan. His fingers gently cupped her and circled her delicate skin. Then he started running his hand down her ribs, lower until his fingers were at the waistband of her shorts. One finger dipped below, tickling her soft belly until she moved her hips slightly, giving him permission to explore further.

He took the opportunity and with just his fingertips pulled her shorts down, exposing her hip bones. She heard him catch his breath and realized he'd seen her bruise.

"It looks a lot better since I put ice on it today." She tried to smile as he looked down at her. Lightning flashed, causing the room to light up, almost making his green eyes flash, so that in her mind, all she had seen was the emerald color sparkle.

His fingers continued on their path, pulling her shorts lower until they were at her knees and he moved aside to pull them all the way off her legs. Then his hands slowly traveled back up her legs, rubbing and touching her skin lightly. She closed her eyes and marveled at the feel of his calloused hands on her soft skin. The cool sheets below her were quickly heating from her skin.

He used his hands on either side of her thighs to spread her legs a little wider. Her eyes shot open and she saw that he was on his knees between her legs, just looking at her.

Her tank top was pushed up and she was almost completely naked. Her hands came up to cover herself.

"No, don't. I want to look at you. You're so perfect. So beautiful. Let me just enjoy you."

Her hands moved back to lay beside her on the bed. What seemed like minutes later, he moved his hands and started running his fingers up the inside of her thigh until she once again closed her eyes and enjoyed the feel of him touching her.

When his fingers reached her most sensitive spot, her shoulders lunged off the bed as she felt sparks shooting behind her skin. One of his hands reached up and held her down to the bed, his fingers spreading wide across her stomach.

"So soft." He ran his finger over her sensitive skin, playing with the moisture there, rubbing it over her lips until she thought she would explode. She gripped the sheets under her and swore it couldn't get any better than having Mitchell touch her private parts.

Then she screamed as his mouth touched where his fingers had just been. Her hands went to his hair, trying to push him away. This couldn't be happening, she thought as she frantically tried to pull him loose.

"Sandi, let me just...mmmmm" He kissed her again and she lost her will to fight him. His fingers ran over her skin as his tongue rolled over her, in her, deeper, until she was screaming again. This time his name was ripped from her lips as he pleased her beyond even her wildest imagination.

When she stopped hearing her heartbeat in her head, she realized he had moved back up near her and was just looking down at her, his head propped up by one of his hands. His other hand was spread wide on her stomach, slowly making circles on the soft skin.

"Mitch?" She asked.

"I know." He leaned down and started kissing her gently. She'd never imagined she would want someone this bad, that the wanting was only half the pain. The need, the desire, the passions went beyond all her imagination.

Using her hands, she rolled him to his back and moved on top of him. Tucking her legs on either side of his hips. Her hands followed the same path his had. Running up his exposed, heated skin as she sat there, looking down at him with only her tank top on. Realizing she was still wearing it, she quickly pulled it up and over her head and it hit the floor. She heard his breath catch.

"So, beautiful." He moaned, and his hands came up and cupped her as her head rolled back and her eyes closed. He pinched her nipples lightly between his fingers and her eyes flew open again. Reaching down, she started running her hands over his muscles. She'd never touched a man before. Did they like the same things she did? Slowly she rolled the tips of her fingers over his flat nipples and saw his eyes closed with passion. Leaning her head down, she ran her tongue over them and felt his hand's fist in her hair gently. She took her time, running her mouth and hands over him until finally, she had moved down to the waistband of his shorts.

Using one finger, she hooked his shorts and started pulling them down off his legs. He gripped her hands to stop her.

"Are you sure?" He asked, looking into her eyes, she nodded her head.

"I want you so bad. I've always wanted you." She whispered.

She used her hands this time and pulled his shorts off. When his erection sprang free from his shorts, she gasped and held her breath. She never imagined that men looked this beautiful, that he'd be this beautiful. Tossing the shorts to the floor, she sat on her knees between his legs and just looked at him.

"Sandi?" He started.

"Ssh, let me just look. Take it all in." She ran a finger down the length of him and he moved with the light touch, causing her to be more interested in his parts. She used both hands to cup him, running her fingers over every inch until finally, he gripped her hands.

"If you keep doing that, you might get a little wet." He chuckled.

She didn't know what he meant by that, but she was ready to move to the next level, she just didn't know what that entailed.

"Come up here." He looked into her eyes and must have seen her questions. She scooted until she was lying next to him, side by side.

"Sandi, have you ever done this before?" He asked.

She shook her head, no.

"I didn't think so. What do you say, we take it slow?" He said against her skin.

She nodded her head and he leaned over and started to kiss her, building her passion back up until she felt she was close to exploding again. Then, his hands moved over her skin. He moved them from her chest to the tops of her legs and back, circling everywhere but where she wanted him to touch again.

She angled her hips towards him, but he seemed determined not to touch her there. Reaching over, she gripped him lightly and felt him freeze in place. He pulled his head back from hers and looked into her eyes; they were both breathing hard as she glided her fingers up and down over the length of him.

Then he finally reached down and touched her, using his fingers to spread her wide before slowly sliding a finger into her as she pleasured him. They matched beat for beat until finally, she felt the explosion coming, she gripped him tighter as he moaned with his pleasure.

After, she didn't really know how long they lay there like that. Finally, after their heartbeats settled and her heated skin cooled, he rolled over and pulled her into his arms.

"I wasn't going to do this, you know," he said into her hair. It was soft and smelled of flowers and he wanted to stay there, wrapped around her, for the rest of time.

"Mmm, I never imagined it would be like this." She sighed.

He wanted to chuckle. He'd thought the same thing. It had never been like this with anyone else, and they hadn't even technically had sex yet. What would happen when they finally came together completely, with no barriers to hold them back? He knew it was the smart thing to wait, but his body was telling him to reach down, pull her leg up and slid into her in one quick motion, burying himself deep in her heat. He closed his eyes and tried to think of something, anything that would stop his cock from rising to full staff again.

Then she moved against him and he lost that battle. His hands snaked around her, pulling her close to him, holding her still.

"Mitch?" She started to move.

"Shh, just let me hold you." He pulled her back.

She snuggled, her back to his front and it was pure torture for him. Finally, she settled her movements down and he lay there breathing in the scent of her hair, feeling her body rise and fall with each breath, until, finally they both slept.

CHAPTER 9

"Why can't I go with you?" Sandi asked.

"We've talked about this. It's too risky. Look at what happened last time you left the building." He gave her a look, and she wanted to pull her hair out.

"That was different, and you know it. This is just a short trip to the market and I'll be with you. You said it yourself, it's just a few blocks away. Besides, my hip is feeling better and being locked in this place is driving me mad." She was trying desperately not to beg.

It had been two days since her run-in with her cousin and the taxi cab and she was going crazy. She'd spent as much time on her art as possible, but she was used to going out, seeing people, being around people. Having to live the way she used to again would kill her. Even though her childhood home was large, and they had four gardens and over thirty rooms, she had always been a prisoner there. She knew that her future husband's family had more wealth than her own and doubted their house would have been anything but more grandiose.

He looked down at her and she saw the moment he changed his mind.

"Fine, but I don't want you to get out of my sight though." He looked at her, a small crease formed between his eyebrows.

She clapped her hands and walked over to grab her new jacket off the coat rack. Then rushed over to the door and closed it behind them as they walked out.

When they reach the lobby, John was helping another tenant move some heavy packages inside. As they walked out the front door, she waved to him as they passed by. He smiled and waved back at her.

"I can't believe you don't know anyone else in your building." She said as they walked along the sidewalk.

"Oh, I know a few other people. It's just that I don't get involved in their lives. I don't know where they work, who their families are, those kinds of things. I stick to my business and they stick to theirs." He said, reaching over and holding her hand.

She shook her head, "You know, I always thought that America was one of the friendliest places on Earth. The first year I moved here I spoke to a total of ten people outside of the women's shelter I lived in. Most of them were my self-defense instructors."

"So, that's where you learned those fancy moves you put on your cousin back there." He smiled at her. She enjoyed walking down the street, holding hands with him. "I was impressed. After my heart started beating again, that is."

She smiled and moved a little closer to him, wrapping her arm around his. "You heard all about Sandi the other night. Tell me something more about Mitchell."

His smile fell away, and she could have sworn she felt him stiffen. "There isn't much to tell. I've already told you about my past."

"No, you told me the bad things about your past. None of the good stuff. Like, where did you go to college?" She asked.

"Princeton. It's in New Jersey. That's where I met Ric Derby. Carter, Eve, and I all attended college there after going to high school together. You can say we had decided early on to stick together."

"Why does Eve have such a problem with Carter?" Sandi frowned a little.

He laughed, enjoying the fact that she could draw the good out of him. "Eve is smarter than Carter and that drives Carter nuts. The fact of the matter is; we should have made her partner a long time ago. The only thing stopping us is that Carter enjoys the hold he has over her."

"Do they hate each other that much?" She asked, looking up at him.

"Oh, I don't think they actually hate each other. Well, you can say they have an underlying appreciation for one other. And they show it, too, when they aren't thinking about killing one another." He laughed again.

She smiled. "I'd like to meet Carter. I've seen the picture of you two on your laptop. You both look very happy."

His smile fell away again, and she remembered the other photos that had popped on the screen.

"I saw the picture of you and Suzanne, too." She looked down at their intertwined hands. Wondering if she was crossing the line. She wanted to know more of what happened between the pair but was trying not to sound too eager for the information.

He stopped at the corner and turned to her. "Suzanne is in the past. I made my mistakes there and it's over. You don't need to worry about that part of my history." He started to walk, but she pulled his hand back until he looked at her again.

"Mitch, I'm not trying to pry. We're molded by our

history into who we are today. I think you know that I haven't been with anyone else like this before. I don't know the rules or etiquette. If I've crossed a line, I'm sorry." She looked down at their hands, waiting.

He moved closer until their noses almost touched, then he put his hands on her shoulders.

"You can ask me anything. I may not always give you the answer you want, but I'll try." He took a deep breath and looked around. "Come with me." He pulled her into a small street cafe where they sat at a booth that looked out towards the busy street. After ordering two coffees, he pulled her hand into his again.

"Suzanne and I met at a business dinner. We didn't hit it off at first. To be honest, looking back at it, that should have been a warning sign. But I suppose I was stubborn. I wanted something with her, and I finally wore her down to where she went out with me. It was just shortly after I'd sobered up, and I was making up for one addiction with another one, by filling my bed with as many women as I could."

He stopped and looked across the table at her. She tried not to show any emotions.

"I did warn you, the truth sometimes sucks." He said.

She smiled slightly. "Continue."

"Well, anyway, I suppose I can be thankful for that long relationship because she broke me of that habit. We started dating, then somehow it was two years later, and I was walking in on her with her lover." He stopped when the waitress refilled their coffee.

"I'm sorry," she said after the young woman left.

"Don't be. To be honest, I think she's happier now. Did I happen to mention that her lover's name was Stephanie?" He said.

Sandi almost choked on her coffee. He moved to her side

of the booth and started smacking her back lightly to get her to breathe.

"I'm sorry." He said, "I guess I should have made sure to say that after you'd swallowed."

She waved her hand in front of her face. Her cheeks had turned a bright shade of pink. She tried to breathe through the heat that had seared her throat. Finally, when she felt like she had her breathing and voice under control, she said, "I'm sorry. I wasn't expecting that. I'm so sorry that happened to you."

She looked over at him and for a second, she thought he was mad. Then he burst out laughing and she followed.

"I guess when you look at it from a different point of view, it really is shocking and funny. You know, when I walked in on them, I actually thought she was giving me a ménage à trois for my birthday." Upon her blank look, he laughed even more. "When two girls please one man."

"Oh! Oh, no!" She looked a little shocked then held her sides. "That's terrible."

"Then why are you still laughing?" He chuckled.

"Because I don't know. Because you are." She smiled across at him and reached for his hand. "Well, I can promise you this, I will never leave you for another woman, or man for that matter."

His eyes dropped, and she could tell she'd said too much, exposed too much of her thoughts. Pulling her hand away, she took another sip of her coffee as she looked out the window, only to come up short and spit her coffee out again, gasping for breath as she stared across the street, right into her father's eyes.

FOR THE SECOND time in the last few minutes, Mitchell moved over and smacked Sandi's back, trying to get her to breathe. This time, he knew it was nothing he said or did that had caused it.

Finally, when she could breathe, she pointed to the window. "My father." Mitchell was up in a flash, he scanned the crowd on the street and didn't see anyone that resembled the image of her father he'd memorized.

"I don't see him." He started to pull her up, noticing her face was even redder than before.

"He was there. Next to the sign," she said between coughs, pointed out the window again. He scanned the crowd a second time. Taking his wallet out, he tossed down a few bills, not caring if he had overpaid.

"Come on, we're leaving." He started pulling her out the door.

"Wait. Mitchell." She pulled on his arm until he stopped. "Where are we going?"

"Home." He started walking again. She pulled him to a stop just outside the cafe.

"No, I'm not going to run and hide every time I think I see my father." She felt like stomping her foot.

"You either saw him or you didn't." He said.

"I did, at least...I think I did. My eyes were teary from all the coughing and laughing." She bit her bottom lip. "I could have been mistaken."

He thought about it. "Well, we'd better be safe rather than sorry. We'll head back and order in."

"No, Mitch. Please. If it was my father, then maybe we can get a look at him if he follows us to the market. We wouldn't want to lead him back to your place."

Why hadn't he thought about that first? When she'd said she'd seen her father, his first instincts were to rush her to safety. Protecting her was his main goal now, and he'd do anything at this point to ensure that she remains safe.

"What makes you think he doesn't already know where I live?"

"I hadn't thought about that." She bit her bottom lip.

"But, you're right." Taking her hand, he started walking towards the market slowly. "No, don't. Keep looking forward," he told her when she moved to look over her shoulder. "Just keep walking. Talk to me. Did you always want to be an artist?"

He could feel the tension in her body, next to his. Squeezing her hand lightly to reassure her, he started swinging their hands playfully. She smiled a little and started talking about when she first knew she wanted to be an artist. He found the story interesting but was paying more attention to the people around him, looking through his dark sunglasses at every movement, every face. When they finished the short walk to the market, he grabbed one of the small hand-held baskets and handed it to her. Then they walked from booth to booth, gathering basic groceries. His mind was so focused on everything else that he accidentally almost bought too many tomatoes.

"Mitch, I think we only need a few tomatoes, not a dozen. Unless you have plans to make enough spaghetti to feed your entire building." She chuckled. He shook his head and set a few back down.

"Sorry, maybe you can focus on the items, so I can focus on the crowd." He suggested.

She nodded, "Have you seen anything yet?"

"No, but there are too many people here to really tell. Let's go over here, they have great bread." He pulled her to another booth.

He came to the farmer's market every week since he

enjoyed the fresh food. He also enjoyed the people he'd come to know and trust over the last ten years of living close by.

"Mitchell!" Rachelle, one of his favorite bakers, who ran the best bread booth in the market, came up and hugged him. At one point shortly before he'd met Suzanne they had tried to date. The relationship had not sizzled, and they had ended up good friends.

"Rachelle, this is Sandi. She's staying with me for a while." He smiled.

He waited as the two women shook hands and sized each other up. He could tell instantly that they liked each other. They began talking about cakes and other items as he tried to scan the crowd. He still hadn't spotted her father, but that didn't mean he didn't believe she'd seen him.

"Mitch?" Sandi was pulling on his arm.

"Hmm?" He looked down at her.

"I was just telling Rachelle that we would love to have dinner with her tonight," Sandi said with a smile.

"Hmm, yeah, sure." He turned to lean against the table and that's when he spotted the man. He was less than half a block away. "Stay with Rachelle." He shouted over his shoulder at Sandi as he started running after him. Instantly the man took off at a fast walk, dodging between people in the crowd until Mitch reached the spot he'd last seen him. Spinning around, he realized that the man had easily disappeared in the crowd. He knew he'd had a slim chance of catching him. Honestly, he didn't know what he would have done if he'd caught him. Maybe shake some sense into him?

At this point, he scanned the crowd again and came up empty. Heading back to Rachelle's booth, he was shocked to see the table tipped over and Rachelle sitting on the ground with people hovering over her.

"Are you okay?" When she nodded and started dusting herself off, he asked. "Where's Sandi?"

"There," she pointed in the opposite direction. "He took her there. Be careful," she yelled after Mitch as he took off running. "He had a knife."

He didn't care if the man had a knife or a gun. He was determined to get Sandi back alive.

CHAPTER 10

"I'm not going anywhere with you!" Sandi tried to pull away again, only to get nicked in her ribs from the sharp blade her cousin held against her.

"Don't worry, we just need to make it back to the car." Sandi saw him nod towards the black sedan he'd been in a few days ago. They were quickly approaching it since he was dragging her with him at an alarming rate.

"Why are you doing this?" she asked, trying to dig her heels in and slow them down. She knew Mitch would be right behind them, all she had to do was stall.

"You know why." He yanked her arm and had them moving quickly again.

"Anish, we used to be friends. Why?" She tried to pull away.

"We've heard you've made quite the name for yourself. You probably have a load of money hidden in some bank somewhere. You need to repay your family for all the trouble you've caused us since you left. Did you honestly think we wouldn't have to pay the Mahabir's back? Everything!

Including taxes. It broke us. I'm going to make sure I get everything you've ever taken away. Before your punishment."

She tried to swing around as he approached the car, but Anish grabbed a handful of her hair. She cried out as he pulled it hard until lights exploded behind her eyes.

Then he was being yanked from her so fast, she lost her footing and landed on her hands and knees. Looking up, she watched as Mitchell plowed his fist into her cousin's face. Anish must have learned how to fight somewhere. The last time she'd seen him, he'd been a skinny kid who couldn't defend himself. Now, however, he was holding his own against Mitchell. She stood up, holding onto the car door to steady herself. The two men circled each other. Anish held the knife out, slashing the air, holding it ready to strike. Just when she thought Mitchell was in trouble, Anish took off running down the street. People scurried to get out of his way as he yelled.

Mitch didn't follow. Instead, he came to her side, running his hands over her. "Are you alright?"

"Yes, shouldn't we go after him?" She asked.

"No, it's just what they wanted. Your father was a distraction, so your cousin could get to you. I should have seen it coming." When he moved his hand to her side, it came back wet with blood. "Damn!" He pulled her jacket aside and untucked her shirt.

"Mitchell!" He was practically undressing her in public. People still stood around, wondering what was going on after the fight they'd just witnessed.

"It's not too bad. You won't even need stitches." He was bent down in front of her, looking at her side.

"I could have told you that. If you'd asked." She pulled her shirt back down and grabbed her jacket from him.

Just then Rachelle came running up. "Is everyone okay?"

"Yes, I think we're both fine," Sandi said, brushing her jacket off before putting it back on.

"Okay, good. Now..." Rachelle turned on Mitchell and pointed a finger at his chest. "Talk!"

"What?" He was busy wiping a small drop of blood from his mouth.

"What was that all about?" Rachelle flung her arms around.

"Why are you asking me and not her?" he pointed towards Sandi.

"Because I know you better than most. We've been friends for almost eight years. You're always getting into messes. Besides, I just met Sandi and she's so sweet, no one could possibly want to hurt her."

"Actually, Rachelle, it was my family that did all this." Her eyes went to the ground. "It's all my fault."

"No," Mitchell walked over and put his fingers under her chin until she looked at him. "We're in this together."

She nodded and smiled slightly at him.

"Well, I've got quite the mess to clean up. I'm glad everyone is okay."

"Rachelle?" She turned and looked back at Mitch. "I'm sorry about all this. I think we'll skip out on the dinner tonight."

Rachelle nodded and turned to walk back to the market.

"What now? It's obvious they've found us."

"Well, first things first. We need to get as far away from here as possible." He took her hand and pulled his cell phone out as they walked to hail a cab.

A while later they were set up at a hotel across from Central Park. Several suitcases were delivered from Mitchell's apartment shortly after they arrived in the lobby. It was all thanks to Carter.

"Do you think we were followed?" she asked as they walked into the single room.

"No, I had the taxi driver take the longest route possible and we both watched for cars following us. Unless they were hovering over us in a helicopter, I think we're safe."

He sat on the bed and removed his jacket and shoes. Then he leaned back on the bed, his arms crossed behind his head. She stood there unsure what to do with herself. She would have never thought her father and cousin would want her money, let alone be after her.

Anish had talked about hard times her family had fallen on after she'd left. She had never thought about what it had cost them for her to disappear like that. She'd always assumed her father and mother had missed her, but never that they would lose everything. A huge wave of guilt hit her, causing her to lean back against the door. She tried to close her mind to it, to the questions she had about her mother, but when she leaned her head back against the cool wood, she couldn't block the images her mind conjured.

Images of her mother, cooking over a small pot in a shack with a thin tin roof, her fingers burned and scarred from the hot stoves. Dirty drinking water, diseases, clothes hanging off her frail body.

She'd seen it all firsthand that first night when Ethan had whisked her away from her emerald palace. Children had played in sewage, coughing, sick, and rail thin. Trash everywhere you stepped. Raw sewage running down the middle of the street. No one should live like that.

The trek through the slums had been one of the main reasons she had donated so much of her income to the shelters. Women and children weren't the only ones getting something from her. Men were being trained for higher paying jobs. Learning different languages so they could work in call centers, so they could care for their families. Or being schooled as mechanics so they could work physical labor jobs.

She'd never imagined how wonderful it would make her feel to give so much back to her people. She'd also donated to the local women's shelter that had helped her when she arrived. She hadn't been back there since the first year, but she could only imagine the good they did with it.

Was her mother benefiting from her donations? For the first time since leaving India, she desperately wished to go back and see how her mother was doing.

"Sandi?" Mitchell's voice broke through her mind.

She opened her eyes and realized he was standing in front of her.

"Let me have a look at that cut." He held up a bottle of antiseptic. "Come over here and sit in the light."

She followed him to the bed and removed her jacket. Her shirt and jacket were cut where Anish's blade had sliced through them.

Mitchell lifted her shirt until the wound was exposed and winced. "Does it hurt?"

She shook her head. "Everything is dull." She meant it, too. Her problems seemed small compared to what her cousin had hinted at.

"What is it?" His face was close to hers. His green eyes searching her own.

"Something my cousin said. Mitchell? Do you think my family suffered when I left?"

He thought about it as he gently cleaned the wound with a cotton ball and antiseptic. "In what way?"

"Financially? Emotionally?" She asked.

"Well, I can't say on the emotional level, but I do know they fell on some hard times after you left." She closed her eyes and a tear escaped, rolling down her cheek. "But not by much. Sandi, from what I learned when I was researching your family, they had to pay back your dowry. As far as I can tell, that was the extent. They didn't lose their house or anything major. Your father's businesses were secure. The harshest thing that happened was when your uncle was found guilty, here in the US. Apparently, he had sent stolen items to your father in India and your father's house was searched. The items were seized. But all of your uncle's properties and belongings were seized, leaving your father to care for your cousin."

"What about my mother?" She was desperately searching his face, hope in her eyes.

"As far as I know she's fine. She is still living in your childhood home."

Sandi closed her eyes and breathed a sigh of relief.

"Sandi, your cousin is warped. He wants to get at you any way he can. I've read hundreds of stories about what men have done all in the name of honor. None of them were justified in my eyes."

He ran his hand over her cheek, wiping the tear away with his fingers. "Don't let him get to you. You did what was right. You stood up for yourself. Many women have never had that chance."

She took his face into her hands and kissed his lips. She tasted the salt from her tears on her tongue. "I owe everything I am, everything I will ever be, to you. I know you would never demand payment, but I want you to know that you have my gratitude and my life." She kissed him again.

He leaned over her, his arms holding him up on the bed as she leaned back against the headboard. She wanted to show him what she felt but didn't know the way to express herself. Funny, she could paint her thoughts, her feelings, but when it came time to show them, she was blocked.

Just then there was a knock on the door. Mitchell jumped up and put his finger over his mouth, signaling her to be quiet. Walking to the door, he looked out the peephole. "Yes?"

"Room service. You ordered dinner for two?"

They *had* ordered food at the front desk when they checked in. She relaxed against the headboard as Mitchell cautiously opened the door. The young woman walked in, pushing the cart with two large silver domes covering their plates. Mitchell tipped the woman and locked the door behind her.

When the savory aroma hit her, Sandi realized she was starving.

MITCH SAT in the room listening to the shower running in the bathroom. His imagination was hard to turn off as he listened, straining his ears to hear every sound. She'd moaned when she'd stepped into the shower, which had set the fantasies starting in his mind. Her. Naked. Water dripping down her sleek body, making her skin glisten as it dripped down her slowly.

He shook his head. Damn, he needed to keep his wits about him if they were going to make it out of this. He'd tried calling Ethan again, this time leaving a more desperate sounding voice mail.

The water turned off in the next room and he wondered why he couldn't stop thinking about her in that way. Why every time she walked into the room, he wanted to touch her. He could hear her moving around and imagined her sliding the towel over her body, drying it. Remembering what she looked like, what she tasted like. He knew there was no way to fight the attraction now, especially since his feelings for her had moved beyond lust.

He knew she had strong feelings for him. It was written

on her face every time she looked at him. He looked up as she walked into the room and when she met his eyes, she stopped brushing her hair. He noticed the red streaks were no longer present in her dark hair. He kind of missed the bright colors.

"If you want to shower...?" She motioned towards the bathroom. He stood up and walked towards her. For a second, he could see desire flash in her eyes, then she blinked and looked down. He smiled and walked by her into the restroom.

He needed to stay focused. He wanted her, but they had too much planning that needed to happen before he could take the time to sort through his feelings for her.

Taking his time in the bathroom, he thought he had come up with a plan when he walked out to find her fast asleep on the bed farthest from the door. Walking over, he turned the light off and crawled in next to her, pulling her close. He needed to hold her in his arms, to sleep touching her, knowing she was safe.

His mind refused to shut down and it took him almost an hour to finally drift off. When he did, the dream started.

Her hands moved over his bare chest slowly, running her fingers up his skin lightly, causing him to moan. She ran kisses along his collarbone as her hands traveled over him. He reached down and found her naked. Touching her skin, he noticed she was still wet from her shower. Her hair smelled of shampoo, and he buried his face in the soft tresses, kissing his way down her neck as she moved her hips against his. Then she was leaning over him, a knee on either side of his hips, her core touching his, causing friction and heat to spread throughout his system.

"Sandi," he moaned, holding her hips still as she moved against him. He couldn't think. He knew he needed something... But, what?

"Mitchell, help me." Her voice was like a shout in the night. He awoke from the dream and bolted upright. He looked around the dark room. Sandi lay next to him, her head turning back and forth with the nightmare.

Gently he scooped her up and woke her slowly, kissing her forehead and talking to her sweetly. He'd never cared so much about someone before. The joy he felt when he realized she'd called to him in her sleep caused his heart to hurt.

Her eyes finally fluttered opened and he looked into her tired eyes.

"Mitch?" she asked.

"Shh, it's okay. The dream is gone now. You're safe." He said against her skin.

"I couldn't find you. Someone was chasing me, and I couldn't find you." She whispered.

"I'm right here. I won't leave you." She sighed and snuggled her head against his bare chest. He enjoyed the feel of her cheek against his skin and started running his hands through her hair.

"Thank you, Mitchell." She said.

"Stop thanking me. I'm not doing this for your gratitude." He felt like groaning.

She pulled back and looked at him. "Why *are* you doing this?"

He thought about it a second. "I suppose it's because I feel guilty. Guilty for getting you into this mess with your family."

She shook her head. "You didn't do anything but save me from a nightmare. If it wasn't for you..."

"Shh. Don't think about it." He closed his eyes.

"How can I not?" She looked up at him. "You say you don't want my gratitude. You keep blaming yourself for the mess my family has caused. I don't know how to show you how much you mean to me." She reached up and cupped his face, bringing it down to hers in a light kiss that seared his heart.

He ran his hands over her and enjoyed the feel of her skin on his. He could have taken her. He wanted to take her. But just then his cell phone rang, causing her to jump.

"Easy, it's just my phone." He reached over and after seeing the number, punched answer. "Yes?"

Thirty minutes later they walked into the hospital. "We're here to see John Alfonso. He was brought in about an hour ago."

They made their way to the room where John was propped up with tubes sticking out of his arms. As they walked in, John looked up.

"You guys didn't have to come all the way down here," he said as a nurse took his blood pressure.

"I wouldn't have heard the end of it if we hadn't come. Sandi demanded it." He smiled as he walked over and shook the man's hand. Sandi slowly approached the man, tears streaking down her face.

"John, I'm so sorry. I didn't know my family would do something like this." She took his hand.

"You had nothing to do with this. I was just doing my job. When I saw that young man sniffing around, I recognized him right off. Mr. Kovich showed me pictures of your family. By the time he approached me, I had already called the cops. They showed up and he took off. I hadn't heard if they nabbed him yet?" He looked at Mitchell.

"I haven't heard either." Mitch frowned.

"Are you going to be alright?" Sandi asked.

"Sure, nothing that a few days off won't fix. Banged me around pretty good, I used to be quite the fighter in my day. That's how I got the job back in eighty-two. The boss comes into the boxing gym where I used to workout. He sees me and Mikie, my little brother. He offers us both jobs right there. I've been working there ever since. Mikie took another job across town to be closer to his kids a few years back."

Sandi had stood and smiled down at John the entire story.

"Well, the only reason I came down to get checked up on was my old ticker here." He pounded his chest lightly. "It isn't what it used to be, and the cops thought I might want to get checked out. No real harm was done. Got myself a nice-looking shiner though." He touched his left eye which was swollen. Then his face sobered. "He got my gun, though. Damn new boss made me start carrying one a few years back. They said it was for extra safety measures." He looked up at them. "The reason I called you two is to warn you that he was asking after Sandi. Kept asking me where she was. Sounded like he knew you weren't staying at your place anymore."

"I'm happy you're okay. I don't know what I'd do if anything bad had happened." Sandi took his hand in hers.

"Don't worry about me none. I didn't tell him anything. Besides, I didn't know where you were, so I couldn't have told him anyway." He smiled a little. Just then the doctor walked in and they excused themselves, saying their good-byes and heading back to the hotel.

When they entered the room, Sandi sat on the unmade bed and looked down at her hands. "Mitch, I think I need to go away so no one else gets hurt. If I can get my hands on my money, I can leave the country and my cousin will never know."

"Until what? One night you're sitting in a hotel and they come knocking on your door? No, Sandi." He sat beside her and took her hand. "We need to find out who is betraying you. How they found you. How he seems to always be one step behind us."

She nodded her head in agreement.

"I know I've asked you this before, but you haven't been in contact with anyone from your old life, correct?" he asked.

"I haven't seen or talked to anyone from Puri since I was two days' shy of my eighteenth birthday. No one from Kovich and Edward Agency knew my real name. All my paperwork and financial records are under my new name, Samantha Rain, which Ethan gave me five years ago."

"Tell me about your art. What projects has Eve had you working on?" Mitch asked.

She thought about it for a minute. "I just finished a project a few months ago for a charity auction. The benefits went to a women's shelter that I stayed in when I first arrived in the States."

"What's the name of the shelter?" He took the hotel pad and pen and started writing out the details of her life.

They spent the rest of the morning going over every tiny part of her last five years. Every project she'd worked on; every charity she'd contributed to. In his mind there had to be a hole somewhere. Now he just needed a computer, so he could find it and seal it up. Then she could start over again, living without fear.

CHAPTER 11

*L*ater that day they took the subway across town to the library. Mitchell didn't let go of her hand once. It was almost as if he was afraid he'd lose her. She'd never been to this library before and when they walked in she stopped to stare at the massive columns and windows.

"Here, this way. The computers are on the next level." He said. They walked up the large stairs and sat down at an empty computer.

"What are we looking for?" She asked quietly.

"I'm not sure yet. I guess we'll know when we find it." He punched a few keys to sign in and went to work, typing and searching from the list they had made earlier. Every event she'd done pieces for over the last five years was listed, as well as the places she had donated money to.

A while later Mitchell found what they were looking for. Apparently, one of her art pieces had been sold to a restaurant in Bhubaneswar, which was just an hour and a half from Puri. The piece currently hung in the main dining hall. Mitchell found a photo of it. Guessing that someone from her family had seen it and recognized it as her work was the first possible lead they'd actually had.

THEY WERE MAKING PROGRESS. At least they thought they were. Leaving the library, they headed back across town. Mitchell received a call from Carter as they were exiting the subway station. Sandi tried to understand what was being discussed, as she watched two kids play in front of a large house. The small boy chased the girl around playfully which caused an old memory to surface. She stood there watching the kids as Mitch talked on the phone and her mind flew to her past.

"Anish, you're cheating," Sannidhi said as she fell to the soft dirt of the garden, her clean skirt getting dirty in the grass.

"I never cheat. You're just too slow. Girls are slower and dumber than boys. Didn't you know that? Oh, I forgot, you're a girl, you don't know anything." Anish stood over her as she pulled her knees to her chest and looked up at him. He was just a year older than her, but she was already taller and outweighed him.

"I'm not dumb." To Sannidhi's six-year-old mind she was the smartest kid she knew, including her cousin. Anish was always picking on her, causing her to fall down. But ever since she'd outgrown him last year, he'd had a harder time at it.

They'd been playing tag in the garden, waiting for their parents to finish a very important meeting when Anish had jumped through the bushes to push her down. He'd cut right across the hedges and now there was a large hole where he'd gone.

"I'm going to tell. Look at me. I was supposed to stay clean and now I'm dirty."

"Who cares? No one cares what you look like, only how much you're worth." Anish said, smiling down at her.

"*What do you mean?*" *She stood up, her little hands balled into fists by her sides.*

"*Don't you get it?*" *Anish smile grew, showing off his crooked tooth in front.* "*They're meeting about your bride's price. There is a family in there that is going to pay your father and mine to take you away, so we never have to bother with you again.*"

Sannidhi fought back the tears. Anish was lying. He always told stories to make her cry. There was no way her father would ever sell her.

"*You're lying!*" *she said and stomped her foot as she put her hands on her hips.*

"*No, I'm not.*" *He smiled bigger.* "*It's called a bride's daw-dy. Or something like that.*"

Sannidhi could tell when her cousin was lying. This time, as she looked into his dark eyes, she saw something that scared her.

"*Why? Why would they do this?*" *She whispered.*

"*Because you're a stupid girl and that's what you are made for. When you get old enough, your family makes money, so you can go cook and please a man. That's all girls are good for. I plan on having several wives like my father does.*" *He crossed his small arms and puffed out his chest.* "*That way I can be pleased all the time.*"

Sannidhi's eyes teared up. "It's not fair." It came out as a whisper as tears fell down her cheeks.

"*Girls don't get fair. They get what men decide they get and nothing more.*" *Anish grunted.*

Sannidhi had heard enough. She took off running towards the white doors, racing to her mother to see if what her cousin had said was true. When her mother confirmed her destiny, Sannidhi never played with her cousin again.

"Sandi?" Her thoughts were interrupted by Mitch's hand on her arm.

"Come on, we're leaving town." Mitch looked worried and upset.

"Why? What's happened?" She asked.

"My office was broken into last night. Files were thrown everywhere. Apparently, your file is missing." He looked over at her.

"What?" She stopped walking and pulled him to a stop. "They broke into your office? Is anyone hurt?"

"No. No one was working last night, but they did quite a lot of damage." He took her hand as they continued down the street towards the park.

"Why are we leaving town?" She asked.

"They could have gotten information off Carter's computer. He made the reservations for our hotel under the business card. If they did a little research, they'd find us. We're better safe than sorry at this point." The hotel was just a quick walk through the park and when they were halfway there, they heard the sirens and saw the smoke. He pulled her to a stop.

"What is that?" She couldn't make sense of the dark cloud over the hotel.

"It looks like the whole building is on fire." They rushed towards the edge of the park, stopping just at the gates to watch the firemen battle the flames that were shooting from the fourth-floor windows.

All eyes were on the flames, but when Sandi looked around, she noticed her cousin standing across the street, looking right at them.

"Mitch, Anish is here." She pointed. A second later, her cousin was darting across the street heading right towards them. Mitch grabbed her hand and yanked her back into the park. They ran along the path eating up as much distance as they could. She looked back and saw her cousin close on their heels. She wanted to turn and confront him but remembered he had John's gun now. She didn't know where her father was either. Was this another trap like the one they had set at the market?

They zigzagged through the park, running down trails she'd never seen or been on before. When they came to the large bridge that crossed the water, they darted to the left down a small pathway instead of going over it.

Here the trees and bushes were a lot thicker. They hit her face and arms as they ran through and after a few minutes of this, Mitchell pulled her behind a large tree and held her against it.

"Shh." He pulled up tight against her. She closed her eyes and tried to control her breathing. A million questions ran through her mind. Had her family set fire to the hotel? She knew they wanted her money, knew they wanted her dead. She knew her cousin and uncle would go to extremes to get their hands on her, but she had always thought better of her father. He'd never once treated her like her uncle and cousin had. He hadn't even treated her mother like she was his property. When she'd found out that her parents had gone through the same thing they had planned for her, it had torn a small hole in her hope. She'd been thirteen and she'd finally built up enough courage to ask her mother how she and her father had met.

"We met as all couples should, on our wedding day." Her mother had told her.

She'd been shocked. Her parents acted as if they loved each other. Her father had always treated her mother with respect and kindness, never treating her like she was his property as her cousin had hinted she would become.

"Do you love each other?" She'd asked.

Her mother had smiled at her. "In our own way, yes."

That answer had never satisfied Sandi. She opened her eyes now and saw that Mitchell was looking at her. His green eyes were inches from her own, his body pressed tight hers as she leaned against the base of the tree, its bark biting into her hands and back.

"I think we've lost them," he whispered next to her ear. She nodded, wanting to ask questions, but she was afraid of speaking. How long should they stay there? Which direction should they go? Where would they go? Why wouldn't he kiss her and end this hunger she felt deep inside.

Her eyes traveled to his lips and back up to his eyes. She watched his eyes travel the same path that hers had. He leaned down and placed a soft kiss on her lips, holding still until she tried to move, wanting more.

He pulled back and shook his head. "Come on, we're not safe here." He took her hand and they quickly made their way through the wooded area until they reached a lit pathway. Here there were other people. Couples walking hand in hand, people riding bikes, families playing with dogs and kids.

She sighed and wished for a piece of that normalcy in her life. Would she and Mitchell ever get to just sit in a park watching the sunset? Would they have children they could take out in public without fear of running into someone from her family? She wanted children. Had always wanted children. But living like she had the last five years, she'd decided against ever putting a child through that kind of hell. Looking over at Mitch as they walked through the park briskly, she wondered if he wanted kids and if he even wanted marriage.

They were approaching the edge of the park, and Mitchell's eyes were everywhere, checking every bush, ever hidden corner. She scanned the people, looking for her father or cousin. When they hit the street, he waved for a cab.

The taxi ride through the city was a long one. Finally, after Mitchell was confident they weren't being followed, they drove to a car rental place, arriving just before dark. She was starved since they had only had small sandwiches for lunch before they'd arrived at the library. While Mitch rented a car she stood there looking into the vending machine, wishing for some change.

"We can do better than some candy bars and chips. We'll stop someplace after we put some ground between us and the city." That ended up being easier said than done since it took them at least another hour to finally make it out of the city and on to the open highway.

"Can you make it a little farther? I know this great place to stop just a few minutes away." She nodded her head and felt like closing her eyes. She'd never been more tired and beat down in her life. Why was this happening to her? She'd never done anything bad in her life, nothing to cause such grief.

"Sandi?" Mitch said.

She looked over at Mitch as he drove. "Yes?"

"I'm sorry about all this. I never thought that when I helped you escape your family that they would go to such lengths to harm you. I never thought past my own selfishness."

"How was your helping me being selfish?" She asked.

"I wanted my hands on your art. All I can say is that when I saw that first piece, the one you had mailed to Singleton, my friend in the UK, I knew you would be something special. When I had Ric Derby contact you and get you to agree to sell several pieces, I knew we had to get you out of India in order for that to happen. The night you called me, I was drunk because Ric had just called, and we'd just heard the final word from your government that they wouldn't allow your art to be shipped outside of India anymore."

"I'm happy things happened the way they did. I wish my father and cousin weren't looking for me, but I'm happy you did what you did." She said.

"I know." He reached over and took her hand. "I'm happy, too. We can stop somewhere and buy us some more clothes, again." He smiled over at her.

"So, this place we're going? It belongs to…?" She asked.

"It was Carter's grandparents' place, now it's his. I don't think anyone will figure out where we've gone. Carter is the only one who knows where we're going. I trust him with my life. The place sits on the end of a cove in a small town in Maine. The nearest neighbor is a few miles away. There's even a lighthouse just down at the end of the bluff."

"I've never seen a lighthouse before, nor have I been to Maine. Do you think I could get some paints? I'd love to paint again while I'm there. You don't have to buy me all the supplies like last time, just some basics." She said, biting her lip.

"Sure, I think they have a shop in town that will have everything you need." He said, smiling over at her.

They stopped for dinner at a small place outside of White Plains. They ate sloppy joes. She'd never had sloppy joes before, and Mitch laughed at her when she tried to eat her sandwich neatly by using her fork and knife. Finally, he had picked his up and shoved it in his mouth and smiled across the table at her, meat and sauce dripping from his face. She couldn't help it, she laughed at him, then picked up her sandwich and did the same.

He'd told her. "The sloppier the joe, the better the joe."

By the time her plate was empty, she had to agree with him. They got back on the road and after an hour of driving and talking, her head started to feel dull. She wished she could see some of the sights since she'd never been anyplace but home and New York City before. Being stuck in a car for a few hours with Mitchell didn't seem like a bad deal to her. Over the last five years, he'd always been the ideal man she'd been searching for in the crowd.

It was hard to explain, but the three days that she'd spent at his place when she'd first arrived in America had been the first time she'd felt free.

Even though her hair had been cut short by Ethan, she had felt like a true woman. She had taken a chance and she was free. Free to be whom she wanted, to live the life she'd always dreamed of. To marry who she wanted.

Looking across the car at Mitchell as he drove, she knew exactly who she'd put in that role.

He was easy to talk to, and the entire drive they talked and laughed with each other. They made it out of Connecticut and Massachusetts quickly and before she could blink her eyes they had passed through New Hampshire. Just inside of Maine, Mitchell pulled into a small motel and stopped.

"Sorry, it's the end of the road for me tonight. We'll catch a few hours and get back to it." He smiled at her. "Stay here."

"I'm not going anywhere." She smiled and watched him run through the light rain that had started when they had entered Massachusetts.

The motel was on the small side and since it was so dark, she couldn't tell how many buildings sat off to the side. They were all painted a dark gray with white and red trim. She supposed it looked very picturesque in the day.

Mitchell strolled back out swinging a key, smiling at her.

"Come on, we can walk from here." He opened the door for her and locked the car.

They walked down a narrow path behind the main building and stopped at the last small building, in front of the last door. She turned and could hear the waves crashing on the beach but couldn't make out anything in the dark. She wished the clouds weren't blocking the moon and starlight, so she could get a glimpse of the view.

"Come on." He waved her in. The place was small and only had one bed.

itchell enjoyed the nervous look on Sandi's face when she walked into the motel room. He didn't know what she had to be nervous about. After all, they had slept snuggled together twice now and he had enjoyed the feeling of lying next to her. Besides, there was no way he was about to get another room just for her. He wasn't going to let her out of his sight.

"Come on, I promise not to eat you alive." He chuckled at the look she gave him. Finally, he took her hand and pulled her into the room, so he could shut and secure it behind her.

Turning back around he realized she hadn't moved. "Why don't you grab a shower first?" He went over and plopped down on the bed, tossing his shoes on the floor. He stretched his arms behind his head and rested back.

By the time she came back out of the bathroom, he was fast asleep.

THE NEXT MORNING when Sandi opened the door, she gasped

at the view. The motel sat on a small hill that overlooked the ocean. She'd seen the ocean a million times in New York, but nothing compared to seeing the beautiful beach and water spread out before her now. The sky was clear, and she could see forever. She felt the cool air hit her face as she stepped outside.

Turning, she looked back at Mitch. He stood leaning against the door jam, smiling at her.

"Do we have time to enjoy a stroll on the beach?" She asked.

He nodded, "Maybe after we grab some coffee and breakfast?"

"That would be wonderful." She smiled.

They stopped at a small bakery and had coffee and bagel sandwiches. By the time they made it to the water's edge, the sun had warmed everything, and the breeze was warm enough that she left her jacket in the car. They walked for a mile, holding hands and talking about the process of how she created her art, then they turned and headed back to the car.

She'd hoped to stop and enjoy some of the other sights along the way, but knew they were on a time schedule. They still needed to stop somewhere and get all the supplies they would need.

She'd been too afraid to ask him how long he planned on staying there. Instead, she chose to imagine they were going to live there, together. Her new life, safe and with the person she'd wanted to share it with.

Almost three hours and a lot of winding roads later, they pulled into the small town of Rockport. Instantly she was charmed by the town, by the old buildings that lined the main street. She'd never seen American architecture like this before. The buildings melted together, starting before the other one ended. She'd heard stories of towns such as this but had never dreamed she would visit one.

Mitch pulled over as she craned her neck to get a better view of the town.

"I thought we'd stop and get our supplies and have some lunch before we head out to the house. The place is just a few minutes from here." He nodded towards the left.

"Oh, yes, please." She opened her door and enjoyed the cool salty air that hit her face. She could get used to living near the water. Puri, her hometown, was on the coast, but instead of quaint little port with colorful boats bobbing in the bay, Puri had a large flat beach with an occasional palm tree. The beaches had always been crowded with people and she'd never truly enjoyed the beauty of it all.

Here, the water's edge was covered with docks and buildings which sat right on them, over the water. The main street was higher up on a hill, so the old brick buildings and street overlooked the bay. You could see to the end of the cove since the sky was crystal clear blue.

"Come on, there's a small general store over here." Mitchell pointed at several buildings to the right. "Then we can eat at Shepherd's Pie, one of the best eateries on the coast of Maine." He pointed to a red brick building with large dark windows and gold letters above. It looked like any place in downtown New York, except its back faced the bay and its front faced the cute little main street of the small town.

They walked down the street and when they entered the general store, a bell chimed over the doorway. An older woman stood behind the counter, helping a woman who had three small kids who were running around, doing everything they could to avoid obeying their mother. Mitchell picked up a basket and started strolling through the aisles, tossing items in it.

She caught up with him and stopped him. "Is this how you shop?"

He looked at her and thought about it. "When I know what I want, I get it. What more to shopping is there?"

She chuckled. "Well, for starters, you picked a pair of socks for three dollars, when there is a bundle of five pairs of socks for just two dollars more." She replaced the socks with the bargain set.

"Why would I need five pairs of socks?" He asked.

"Well, I don't know. How long did you say we would be staying here?" She returned.

He thought about it. "Good point. I guess I don't know. What else do we need?" He took her hint and slowed down. They took their time walking aisle by aisle until they had a full cart of items they both needed.

"The grocery store is a few doors down. We'll wait and stop there after lunch." He paid the woman with cash and they piled their bags back into the trunk of the rental.

"It was smart of you to grab the cash. I wish I would have had access to my money," Sandi said as they loaded the bags into the back. "I know my family is after it, but it would have been nice to not feel like I owe you everything."

"Sandi, you don't owe me anything." He took her hand.

"I know. It's just that—" She started.

"No, don't. You don't have to pay me back." He said, looking down into her eyes.

She looked into his eyes and saw that he was getting irritated. Nodding her head, she squeezed his hand. "You're right. I'm just a little hungry. Shall we eat lunch?"

They walked across the street and went into the charming building. She immediately wanted to sketch the place and the people in it. She normally didn't lean towards drawing people and buildings, but something just called to her. They walked across the dark wood floors that creaked under their feet and sat by the long bar; where the chefs stood behind in plain sight, making their masterpieces.

Sandi ordered the grilled cheese and Mitchell had some shepherd's pie. She was a little leery about what a shepherd's pie was, but when the dish was served, it looked delicious. Mitch had even given her a few bites. She decided then that if they ate there again, she would get the dish the next time.

The atmosphere seemed friendly and they ended up talking to the chef behind the counter for a while. She tried to hide her surprise when Mitch told the man that they were husband and wife, staying at an old friend's place on the cove. She would have coughed again, but thankfully Mitch chose to wait until she'd swallowed the drink first before lying to the man's face.

When they walked out, Mitch turned to her and kissed her right on the doorstep. She felt a little embarrassed, and when he held her hand and they strolled down the street towards the market, he chuckled.

"I had to hold up our appearances. I thought it best that if anyone asks, to say that we're on our honeymoon staying at a friend's. They don't need to know the particulars. If someone were to come asking after us, it might throw them off the trail."

They strolled through the small mart and grabbed everything from shampoo to fresh fruit. He said he didn't know what was in the house, since the last time he'd visited was when Carter and he had graduated college, years ago. He told her the place was huge and had been well stocked the summer he had stayed. She still didn't know what to expect.

She found a supply of colored chalk, watercolors, and colored pencils. It was a lot like you'd use in school, but she could work with it. There were different sizes of sketch pads and she grabbed one of each size, knowing this would keep her entertained while they were in hiding.

Driving the winding road to the end of the cove, she enjoyed the sights. She'd never been somewhere so green before. Even the sky looked bluer than before. She itched for her oil paints and a blank canvas. When the road turned to dirt, Mitch slowed down as they bumped down the unused road.

"I think the last time Carter was here, was a few summers ago. I know he has a neighbor watching the place. I thought at one point he had a cousin living here."

They pulled around a sharp corner and when Sandi saw the massive house for the first time, she gasped.

"We're staying there?" She said, pointing to the massive house.

"Yeah. It's kinda big isn't it?" He chuckled.

The large, three-story gray building had white trim and a bright red door. It sat near the edge of a small rolling hill that overlooked the water. The trees and bushes that surrounded the place were neatly trimmed and maintained. The white shutters on every window looked brand new, and there was an American flag flying near the front porch.

"Are you sure this is the right place?" She leaned forward, trying to get a better look as they pulled up.

"Yes. It looks like Carter *has* had someone taking care of it." Just then an older gentleman stepped out and waved. "Hang on, let me do the talking."

Sandi nodded her head and stayed in the car as Mitch got out and shook hands with the man. A few minutes later Mitch walked back to the car smiling.

"That was the neighbor, Mr. Johnson. He lives up the road. Apparently, he's been taking care of the place for Carter. Carter phoned ahead and asked him to get the place ready for us." Mitch opened her door and helped her out as the older man drove back down the lane in his truck, honking and waving as he went. "He's stocked the place, even made sure there was gas for the boat." Mitch smiled. "I always loved going out on the water when I was here before."

She'd never been on a small boat before. If it was anything like the large tanker she'd taken to America with Ethan five years ago, she'd rather stay on land. They stood there and looked up at the house.

"What are we going to do with this much room?" She put her hands on her hips as he laughed. She turned to him. "What?"

"Nothing." He shook his head and walked around to open the trunk. "Let's get these supplies in and then I'll give you the tour around."

She'd thought the place was huge on the outside. When they walked in the back door and entered a huge kitchen, she realized it was bigger than she had imagined. She unpacked the supplies and put them away as Mitch ran back and forth bringing more in from the car. When he'd bought the last bag in, she asked. "You said Carter's grandparents lived here?"

"Yeah, his grandfather built the place when all their kids were young. Carter's mother came from a large family of eight. Most of them are gone now since his mom was the youngest. She lost two brothers in Vietnam, a sister died in a fire shortly after she was married. The rest are scattered around the globe. The house was left to his mom and when she died a few years back, the place went to him. He doesn't get up here as often as he wants since our office is in the city."

"Why don't you move your offices here?" She was busy looking out the large kitchen bay windows that overlooked a large side yard and didn't quite hear what his reply was. "I'm sorry?" She turned back to see him standing right behind her.

"Hmm? Oh, sorry. It's easier to meet the needs of our clients in the city. But I suppose there isn't a reason why we couldn't have a branch somewhere else. We've grown big enough. Actually, I've been thinking of branching off. Maybe moving out of the city." He was looking at her and she got the impression his mind was elsewhere.

"Well, how about that tour now?" She grabbed his hand and started pulling him into the next room.

They walked into a large dining area and the huge table reminded her of home. It must have sat between ten and twelve people. The wood shined like new. The chairs needed a little work, maybe some new upholstery, but other than that the room was pleasant.

They walked by a bathroom that was navy blue, that she thought could use some updating. There was a smaller office that was just inside the main hallway off the front door area.

Then they moved into a large living area. The windows overlooked the water and she could see for miles. Here, the furniture was older and out of date with their mauve flowered designs, but the room had potential. As an artist, she could see all that was basically needed was some updated paint, drapes, and furniture. There was a piano that sat in an alcove of windows.

There was a grand staircase—at least that's what Mitch called it—that twisted in the middle of the house and went all the way up the three floors. You could see the railing of the stairs and landings if you looked up. All three floors were open. At the top was a frosted, circular window that let all the light float down the large opening. The cool wood railing shined under her hands and the smoothness mesmerized her.

On the first level, there were four small bedrooms, two bathrooms, and a laundry room. They climbed the stairs again and here there were two larger rooms on the left, each with their own bathroom, and to the right was the master bedroom with a huge bathroom attached.

The place was only half the size of the house she'd grown up in, but she enjoyed the cozy feeling over the open spaces. She could just imagine a family of eight living here. Kids running up and down the stairs, screaming at each other as they played.

She'd always wanted a lot of children. Maybe because she'd been an only child?

"What are you thinking about?" Mitch asked, taking her hand and walking back down the stairs.

"Kids." She said easily.

He coughed and almost missed a step.

"Oh, not our kids." She chuckled, trying to cover her embarrassment. "The kids that had grown up in such a wonderful house."

He smiled a little. "How about a walk along the beach?"

"That sounds wonderful." She wanted to see the water. She wanted to paint it, but she would settle for a nice stroll, hand in hand with Mitch.

$\mathcal{M}$itch's mind was going a million miles an hour as they walked along the shore. He thought Sandi was probably thinking about art, wanting to paint or sketch the scenes she was seeing. Her eyes darted everywhere. He could see she wasn't missing a thing as they walked slowly along the small sandy beach. There were large dark rocks at either end of the cove, protecting it from adverse weather. They made it to a little inlet and sat on a piece of driftwood, each of them quietly sitting, looking off into the distance.

"You said there was a lighthouse?" She asked a few minutes later.

"Yes, it's the other way down the beach." He pointed to the end of the cove. "It's a little longer walk. We can take it when we have a little more time."

"I've never seen one. There is so much in life I've missed out on. So much I've been afraid to do since arriving. I thought that by hiding in a city of eight million, that I'd be safe. I was wrong."

He could see where the sense of security would come

from having people around you. Feeling like there is so much going on that you couldn't help but blend in. But he also knew that there could be safety or danger everywhere you went.

"What kind of things do you want to do?" He asked.

She looked off and watched a boat that was slowly making its way around the cove, heading towards the bay. "Well, I'd like to visit some places I've read about. We traveled through some of them when Ethan helped me escape. But we did a lot of traveling at night and I couldn't see the landscape or experience the people and cultures. I've always wanted to see the Great Wall of China, the Grand Canyon, San Francisco, and some other places like those. Have you ever jumped out of a plane?" She turned and looked at him.

He laughed. "No, I've never had that desire. I have a healthy fear of heights."

"Oh," she turned and looked a little disappointed.

"Do you want to jump out of a plane?" He asked.

"No, but I'd love to talk to someone who has. See what it feels like. Ethan said he did, but he wasn't very easy to talk to." She frowned.

He laughed. "Ethan can be very hard to talk to at times. Especially when he's working. That was one of the main reasons for our friendship."

"I didn't hear how you two met." She leaned forward, putting her face into her hands as she leaned on her knees.

Mitch laughed again. "That in itself is another funny story. It seemed we dated the same girl."

Her eyebrows shot up. "What's so funny about that?"

"Well, we were dating her at the same time." He chuckled again. "Apparently he'd been in New York for a while on an undercover job. This was when he still worked for the military. He'd been stationed there for over three months and had started dating Krista shortly after arriving. Krista and I had met at a club one night when I was still in school, and I thought we'd hit it off. We'd gone out a few times and I thought things had taken a turn towards the serious. Apparently, she'd forgotten and set up a date with the both of us at the same time. Well, when we showed up, flowers in hand at her doorstep, she'd laughed and casually asked us both in. Ethan looked at me. To be honest, I thought of turning and running away as fast as I could, but then he laughed. We both turned and walked away. We ended up talking in the parking lot for an hour and have been friends ever since. I didn't find out what he did for a living for a few years."

He stood and stretched his arms over his head. Taking a deep breath. He enjoyed the fresh, salty air here. He watched as birds flew close and thought of bringing some bread next time to toss to them.

"Well?" He turned back towards her, holding out his hand. "Shall we go try and figure out what we'd like for dinner?"

She smiled and when he pulled her up, he took his time and saw her eyes heat as he pulled her close. The mood called for light and playful, but when their mouths touched, he couldn't hold back the desire that slammed into him when he tasted her.

Her hands went into his hair and he moaned when he felt her clenching him, holding him to her. He could feel her heartbeat against his chest as he ran his hands up and down her sides. She'd worn her light jacket and as he unzipped it to get his hands on her, she leaned her head back, exposing her soft neck for his taste.

Taking his time, he ran his mouth over her cooled skin as his hands moved in her coat, under her shirt, until he could feel her skin under his hands. He wanted her, wanted her worse than he'd ever wanted before. He'd been patient since he knew she was inexperienced, but he was at the end of his rope. He had to have her soon. There was no denying the attraction and the desire they both felt when they were around each other.

He traced her ribs as he ran his hands up her sides until finally, he cupped her gently, causing a moan to escape from her mouth. He covered it with his own moan as her hands were busy traveling over his shoulders, kneading and pulling him closer.

"Mitch? I don't know how much longer I can wait." She said against his skin.

"Are you sure? I know you've never..." He started.

She covered his mouth with her finger. "It doesn't matter. Nothing matters anymore but being with you."

He smiled down at her and for a minute he could imagine they were the last two people on the face of the earth. No rules to be broken, no taboo marks against them. They could share their passions and not be riddled with guilt or labels. They could be free to live and be with whom they wanted. Each other.

He reached down and took her hand in his and started walking back to the house, quickly.

When they reached the house, he helped her remove her jacket and she shivered at the light touch. He knew he had to make this night perfect. Even if she didn't know what she wanted, he knew he had to give everything to her.

"Go up, take a hot bath. There's a jet tub in the master bathroom. I'll cook us something and bring it up." He smiled and kissed her gently on the lips. He could see the decision and the relief in her eyes. She nodded and walked out.

He looked around and found a bottle of champagne, he put it in the freezer to chill while he cooked grilled salmon and new potatoes with spicy green beans, one of his favorite and best meals. He found a stockpile of candles, no doubt left there in case of power failure. Piling them on a tray with a bucket of ice and the champagne, he carried them upstairs into the master bedroom. He could hear her in the bathroom, still in the tub as he set the candles around the room and lit them all. Then he turned the lights down low and went back downstairs to get the trays of food.

When he returned, she was sitting on the edge of the bed, dressed in a white silky tank top and see-through lacy underwear. He almost dropped the tray of food when he saw her.

She looked nervous as she sat there, biting her bottom lip, looking at him across the room. He set the trays down on a small table and crossed the floor to her, the food and champagne forgotten as he took her hands and pulled her to her feet. He stood back and just looked at her. His eyes ran up and down her body. Her perky nipples poked through the light material and he could see dark circles through the soft see-through material. He could see her bruise from the taxi cab incident; it was lighter and less defined.

Then his eyes traveled down her flat stomach, to where the small patch of lace covered the dark triangle of hair that covered her sex. His eyes stayed drawn on her until they almost watered. Then he blinked and looked down, taking in her long, smooth legs. Her skin was dark and seemed to shine in the candlelight. He knew she'd be soft if he touched her, but held back, wanting to see everything. When his eyes traveled back to her face, he realized she was waiting nervously for his response.

"Beautiful. I never imagined." His voice was hoarse as he looked at her face. Her dark eyes glowed in the candlelight. She had a slight smile on her lips and he noticed that she'd found some make-up. At least her lips shined like she had gloss on and her eyes were darker, causing them to stand out more.

Moving slowly, he stepped closer, removing any space

between them, her almost-naked body next to his fully clothed one. Her arms went over his shoulders, his hands to her hips, pulling her tight against his desire. He watched her eyes light up and then cloud over. Grinding her hips against his, she closed her eyes and moaned, leaning her head back. He took the opportunity to dip his head and use his mouth on her long, slender neck. She smelled like heaven and tasted even better. Her hair was still wet, falling in light waves down her back. Pushing his hands into it, he marveled at the softness as he gripped it in his fist and feasted on her heated skin.

She pushed his shirt up until he stepped back and quickly disposed of it, tossing it to the ground. He watched as her eyes sparkled when she looked at him. Then she stepped closer and ran her hands over his arms and chest.

"Impressive. When I first saw you last week, in just that towel, I knew I wanted my hands on you. I've never seen a man or touched him like this." She ran her fingers over his skin lightly, setting off fires that traveled straight to his groin. He closed his eyes and moaned, knowing he had to stay focused so he could go slowly and give her pleasure.

Reaching up, he took her wrist and moved her hands behind her back. "Let me. I want to show you everything you've ever dreamed of. Just let me." He dipped his head and took her mouth in a gentle kiss. Then he walked her back a step until her knees hit the edge of the bed. Using his hands under her arms, he moved her so that she was lying underneath him on the soft mattress. Her damp hair fanned out on the soft comforter. Looking down at her, he swore something shifted as her eyes showed her soul and all of her emotions. He'd never trusted like this before. He knew he'd never trust like this again.

Slowly, with his eyes on hers, he ran his fingers up her sides, pulling the silk tank-top up with them, until finally, she was exposed to his view. His eyes left hers and traveled over her skin until she arched, and his hands cupped her on their own free will. Her dark nipples puckered, begging for his mouth to explore. He dipped his head and when her hands went to his hair, he lapped up every inch of her until she was writhing under him.

He'd wanted to go slow but hadn't counted on her reaction to him. When his mouth moved lower to play over the lace that covered her, her legs spread, and she gripped his head, holding him closer. Gently, he soaked the lace with his mouth, running his tongue over the heat until he traced her lips through the light material. Then, using one finger, he pulled it aside and set his tongue to her heated skin. She screamed his name as he slid a finger slowly into her.

He couldn't wait any longer. He'd come prepared. Grabbing a condom from his back pocket, he stood up and had his pants off quickly. Sheathing himself, he stood there looking down into her dark eyes. When he realized she was looking at him, he stood there and let her get her fill. Her eyes traveled over his arms, down his chest and stomach until finally she looked at him, fully ready for her soft body.

"Don't be afraid." His voice cracked as he knelt between her legs, using his hands to spread them wider.

"I'm not. I've wanted this, wanted you my whole life." She smiled, and he could see the fear leave her eyes. Bending down, he kissed her slowly as he moved and started to slide into her. She was tight, and he tried to maintain his slow speed. When he reached her barrier, he held still as long as he could, letting her get used to his weight and length. But then she moved her hips, rotating them as her hands came to knead his hips. In one quick move, he took her as she screamed his name.

SANDI SMILED and looked up at the ceiling as the candlelight flickered across the cracks in the plaster. Mitchell's weight pinned her to the soft mattress, and she could feel his heartbeat and his breath on her chest. She didn't mind that she was completely naked with a man who wasn't her husband. She didn't mind that he was ten years older than her and not of her religion or race. She didn't even mind if there was no real future in their relationship, although thinking about this caused her heart to skip a beat. The passion they had given one another was all that mattered now. That, and knowing there would be more where that came from.

She'd lived more and done more since she'd been with him than she had in the last five years of her life. For that matter, more than she'd ever done before. She felt alive. Sure, there was a soreness spreading between her legs, but it only made her feel more alive, more aware.

Her fingers were buried in Mitch's hair. She enjoyed the slight curl, running her fingers around the softness of it. He was still inside her and she could feel him growing again. She had so many questions to ask him but felt too embarrassed to voice them. How long before they could do it all again? How many times? What was the small package he'd used before?

She had no experience with sex or the opposite sex. Her mother had never had "the talk" as Americans called it. She'd heard about protection on the television, but the commercials never explained how it worked. She'd assumed that's what Mitch had used but wanted to know more. She wanted to see what he looked like when he wasn't engorged and swollen.

"What? I can hear your brain working, you know." He chuckled into her hair.

"You'll think I'm silly." She turned her head and placed a kiss above his ear.

"Right now, you could probably ask me anything, and

trust me, I won't think it's silly." He buried his face further into her hair, breathing deeply. "I love the smell of you." He started running kisses up her neck. Causing her eyes to close with pleasure. "Ask me anything." He said between kisses.

"What was that thing you used?" She felt her cheeks heat and turn red.

He pulled back, holding himself above her with his arms. "When?"

"Before... Before you..." She closed her eyes and turned her head. His fingers moved under her chin, pulling her face back to his. When she opened her eyes, he was smiling down at her.

"Are you talking about the condom?" He asked.

She shrugged her shoulders. He pulled back. Reaching down he took another packet from his back pocket. "This?" When she nodded, he smiled. "It's a condom. It's protection against getting you pregnant or transmitting diseases." Upon her look, he balked. "Not that I have any. God. No, I get checked twice a year. Besides, I haven't been with anyone since Suzanne, and even then, it was almost half a year since we'd..." He looked away and it was his turn to be embarrassed. Then he stood up and pulled her with him. "Why don't you go in and clean up, then we can have some dinner."

She looked down at herself and realized there were dark stains on her thighs. She rushed to the restroom, more embarrassed than before.

She'd heard about her virgin blood but had always assumed since she was older, that it wouldn't have been that bad. She was thankful she'd left her other new clothes in the bathroom and quickly donned a pair of yoga pants and another tank-top, this one the color of Mitchell's eyes. When she walked out, he was sitting on the side of the bed waiting for her.

"Everything okay?" he asked.

She noticed the comforter was pulled back and the bed was turned down. He wore a pair of new shorts he'd bought from the store. Nodding her head, she walked over and sat next to him. When he walked over to grab her tray from the table, she laughed when she noticed that the word Maine was stretched over his butt in bright white letters.

"What?" He looked at her.

"You have Maine on your butt." She pointed.

"What?" He looked at her funny now and she laughed even more.

"Maine. It's on your backside." Holding the tray of food, he turned around, trying to see the lettering on his back. He looked like a dog chasing its tail, trying to see it. She laughed even more. He stopped and smiled at her, and she knew he was just messing around.

Then he walked over and looked down at her. "Here, sit with your back against the headboard." When she moved into position, he set the tray of food across her lap. "For tonight, we'll eat in bed while watching a movie. I hope you like mystery and comedy. I found this." He walked over and held up a video titled, "Clue."

"I love mystery and comedy." She smiled. "This food smells wonderful." He bent over, turned on the set, and put the movie in the old VCR.

"I hope this works. It looks like this hasn't been used since the eighties." He grabbed the remotes and his own tray then sat next to her.

"I feel like a kid. Eating dinner and watching movies in bed." He smiled over at her. "Oh!" he said, pushing off from the bed. "I almost forgot." He walked over and took the champagne and two glasses from the table. Pouring some in each glass, he handed her one.

"I've never had this before. What is it?" She asked after taking a sip.

"Champagne. It's for special occasions. I found a couple of bottles in the pantry. Here." He held up his glass. She held up hers the same way and he clinked them together. "To old movies, great food, and great sex." He smiled.

By the time the movie had started, her plate was half empty and she'd gone through her first glass of champagne.

CHAPTER 14

The next morning, the sun and birds woke her from a deep sleep. She was snuggled against something very warm and hot breath was on her neck, causing her to almost sweat. Trying to move, she realized she was being pinned down by Mitchell's weight.

"Mitch?" She tried to push him aside, only to have his arms snag around her waist. Pushing harder, she laughed as he buried his face in her hair. She knew what he'd see if he opened his eyes. Her hair was probably standing in spikes around her face. She desperately wanted to run to the bathroom to straighten herself up and brush her teeth.

Finally, she freed herself from his arms by pushing herself away from him, only to land on the carpet by the bed. Looking up, she saw him leaning over the edge of the bed, his chin resting in his hands as he smiled down at her.

"Going somewhere?" He asked.

She raised her chin and started to stand. "Yes, I was heading to the restroom so I wouldn't knock you out with my morning breath. But since you've made it difficult, maybe you deserve my dragon breath." She started to move towards him, only to end up back on the bed with him hovering over her.

"Hmmm. I doubt you have dragon breath, let's see." He dipped his head and tasted her lips. "Nope, you taste like champagne bubbles. Sweet." He licked her lips and she lost her will to fight when his tongue darted out and played with hers. Her hands went into his hair and she realized she could spend the whole day in bed with him. She no longer felt shy when he pulled her shirt up and over her head. His eyes traveled over her bare skin and she felt the heat spreading throughout her entire body.

He'd slept with just his shorts on and she enjoyed running her hands over the smoothness of him. When he leaned down and took her mouth, the light covering of hair on his chest brushed up against her and she felt a new sensation. Wrapping her legs around his hips, she pressed herself to him and marveled in the feel of him hardening. She rubbed herself against him, loving the way his hips pumped against her. When she reached around to pull him closer, he pulled back and quickly shed his shorts, then in one quick swipe, removed her clothes. She started laughing, then seeing his face, she stopped and almost moaned. Desire and passion flooded his green eyes, making them almost shimmer.

Slowly he reached over and took the foil package off the nightstand. He opened it and showed her the small see-through disk, then rolled it on himself slowly, allowing her to see exactly what he was doing. She found it both interesting and exciting to watch his movements. He moved back onto the bed and smiled down at her.

"Is there anything else you'd like to know?" He asked.

She shook her head and closed her eyes as he slowly entered her. He ran kisses up and down her neck, causing goose bumps over every inch of her skin.

"Wrap your legs around me again and hold on." He held

himself above her and she did what he asked until he was thrusting faster, and she found it hard to catch her breath between the want.

"Come with me." He whispered in her ear as he thrust one final time and they both exploded together.

***

MITCH SAT on the beach watching Sandi paint with her new watercolors. He'd brought along a book that he had found in the house but found it boring and uninteresting. Instead, he spent his time watching her. Her movements were swift and sure as she used the brushes on the large canvas they had purchased. He knew she could easily spend the whole day painting without a break, but the dark clouds heading their way told him they had another hour before they would end up getting wet. It was just past lunchtime when he heard the first thunder and finally walked over to her, and they packed up her supplies. They walked in the back door five minutes before the rain started.

The whole house seemed darker once the clouds loomed overhead. They turned on the lights, but the false lighting gave the house a different atmosphere. The place was meant for natural light. They found a few older games in a cupboard and since Sandi had never played Monopoly before, he spent half an hour teaching her, only to have her kick his butt in the game. She ended up with more houses and hotels then he'd ever had playing the game.

"I guess I have a mind for numbers. I noticed it when I got my first paycheck, the very first money that I had earned on my own." She smiled. "It was invigorating knowing that I could support myself." She sat cross-legged on the ugly yet comfortable couch in the large living room. The rain continued to pelt down while the thunder crashed. At one point he thought they might lose power, but it flashed on and off a few times then remained steadily on.

"We never did get to log in to your bank and check your accounts." He said.

"That's okay, I don't think they could get their hands on it. There are passwords even they couldn't break. Besides, they would have to know my bank and account numbers. I didn't have them written down anywhere. I do all my banking online and make sure everything is secure, something Ethan taught me before he left."

"Really? Why would he do that?" He asked.

She took a deep breath. "Because the night he came and rescued me, he hacked into my father's accounts and stole my dowry. He moved every penny of it into a secure account for me." She looked off into the window, not really seeing the darkness of the day. "It's something he told me about once we'd made it to the boat. He told me my family had ten times that amount and after the hell they'd put me through, I deserved it." She smiled and looked at him. "I didn't know they would have to pay it all back." Her smile fell away.

"Sandi, it's not your fault. Like I said, as far as I can tell your family is no worse off than before you left." He said, reaching over and taking her hand.

She nodded. "I don't doubt it. I haven't even touched that money. To be honest, I don't know if I ever will. I've made a good living off my paintings. Enough that I could live comfortably and still give a good chunk to any charity of my choosing. If my family had come to me and asked me for the money back, I would have given it to them freely."

He moved closer to her and kissed her forehead, running his hands through her hair. How could someone be so generous? After all her family did to her, she was still willing to be kind to them. She amazed him. He'd never known anyone so selfless.

"I have a few other games I can teach you to play." He smiled against her mouth, walking her backward towards the stairs. She laughed and wrapped her arms around his neck. In one move she was in his arms as he carried her up the stairs.

Later he made a fire in the downstairs fireplace. There was enough wood stacked up by the back door that he didn't have to venture out to the larger pile that was getting wet in the downpour. The storm was gaining strength and the wind was blowing pretty hard, chilling the large place. Sandi was snuggled up on the couch, tucked beneath a heavy blanket wearing her jacket, a hot cup of coffee in her hands.

"The first winter that I lived in New York, I thought I'd freeze. I'd never been anywhere where it snowed before. I remember when I was younger, one winter it actually got below ten degrees Celsius and I thought that was cold. But that first winter here, I think it hit five degrees. The snow was so much fun that first year. I can remember walking out and seeing it for the first time." She closed her hands over her coffee cup, trying to warm them. "I didn't own any winter clothes, so naturally I was grossly under-dressed, but I didn't mind. I walked to the park and played with a few children, throwing snowballs until I couldn't feel my fingers. Then I went home and took a hot bath." She sighed. "I still can't get used to the cold, but I don't mind it. It's such a nice change."

"Wait until you see the fall colors up here." He thought about it. "You know, in the next few days, I bet we see the leaves start to change. I could take you on a drive, show you some beautiful places I know. There's this church I know of. I bet you'd love to paint it." He suggested.

"Oh!" She sat up a little, "That sounds wonderful. I've seen some photos of this part of the country, I've always wanted to paint up here."

He smiled. "How about we take a drive tomorrow if the weather holds?"

"I'd like that." She was smiling at him as a flash of lightning lit up the sky. He was standing with his back to the window, but when her face showed signs of horror, he spun around and scanned the darkness behind him.

"What?" He rushed towards her.

"Mitch, there's someone out there by the woodpile." She sunk back into the couch, trying to make herself smaller.

He spun towards the windows, looking into the darkness. He waited for another flash of light, but the sky was dark. Walking towards the back door, he grabbed his jacket.

"Wait!" She jumped off the couch. "You can't go out there!" She grabbed his arm.

"Why not? Sandi, we don't know if it's your family. It could be a neighbor, or someone lost. I'm just going to take a look." He walked to the kitchen cupboard and grabbed the flashlight he'd seen earlier. Checking to make sure it worked, he walked to the door. "Lock this behind me."

She nodded, and he walked out into the darkness.

SANDI WATCHED MITCH WALK OUT. She wanted to scream. Why would he go out there? What could he do? She stood by the back door, looking at the beam of light coming from the flashlight as he looked around the yard. She could see him head to the woodpile where she'd seen the dark figure minutes before.

She craned her neck trying to get a better view, and he disappeared around the large pile. The flashlight beam disappeared for minutes and she held her breath, listening for any sounds as the rain pelted against the door. Rushing over to the window, she hoped to see the light, but the yard was dark, and she started panicking even more. What could she do? Should she run out there? She knew the phones weren't working in the large house, so calling for help was out of the question.

Just when she thought of running and opening the back door, yelling for Mitch, she saw the beam of light off to the left, by the car.

Rushing to that side of the house, she watched the light follow the pathway around the house. Each time she ran to another window to watch Mitch searching the yard. It took him almost twenty minutes to complete a sweep of the yard. When he walked up to the back door, she was there to unlock it. Questions pouring from her.

"Hang on," he said, shaking the water from his hair. He scraped the mud off his shoes and tossed them on the tile floor, where they sat dripping with mud and water. He hung his jacket on the hook by the back door and rubbed his hands together. "I could use some coffee."

She rushed to the coffee pot and poured him a full cup. She realized her hands were shaking as she handed it to him as he sat at the table. She sat next to him, watching his face, waiting for news.

"I couldn't see anything. No footprints in the mud, no tire tracks along the driveway. I walked around the whole place and found no signs that there was anyone out there. Are you sure you saw someone?" He took another drink of his coffee and rubbed his hands together.

She nodded and felt like crying. Maybe she was losing it? Closing her eyes, she rested her head on the table. A memory flashed in her mind and she could clearly see the dark image standing by the wood pile. "Someone was there. I know it."

"Okay, I believe you. Well, whoever it was, we must have scared them off. It could have been some kids or maybe a neighbor checking out the lights from the house. The place has been empty for years, then all of a sudden we have every light in the place on and smoke coming from the chimney. Someone was bound to notice and be curious about it."

It sounded reasonable. After all, if it had been her family, she doubted they'd be hiding out in the rain in the dark. It just didn't seem like their style. Her cousin took action, and her father... She closed her eyes and sighed. She missed her father and still hoped he wouldn't have been part of something like this.

Mitchell's hand touched hers, and she realized how cold it was. "Sandi? Why don't we head upstairs? I'd like to take a hot shower to warm up."

"Oh, you must be chilled. Your hands are like ice cubes." She took them in hers and rubbed them to bring some warmth into them.

He smiled at her. "I know a few tricks to getting warmer faster."

She smiled at him. "I know a few as well."

He got up quickly and made sure the back door was locked, then walked in and shut the glass doors on the fireplace. Taking her hand, they walked up the long stairway together.

When they entered the bathroom, he started peeling his wet clothes off, dropping them on the tile floor. When he was naked, he turned to her. She'd been watching his striptease, enjoying the play of his muscles as he moved. His skin glowed in the light and when she placed her hand on his chest, she realized the contrast between their skin colors.

Her hand was dark and small on his chest. He stood very still as she ran it down his tight stomach, past a very tight six-pack of muscles that played across his belly. She moved and walked around him, running her hand over his ribs, around to his back, lightly touching him. He rolled his head back and moaned. She continued her circle of him, running her hands lower across his perfect butt. She gripped each cheek and lightly dug her nails into them, knowing he'd enjoy the feeling. Then she was back around to his front and her hands were on his hips, her eyes on his face. Desire so strong flashed in his green eyes, she almost took a step back.

"You bewitch me." His voice was husky and laced with passion. She stepped back and slowly started peeling her own clothes off. He stood there, naked, his hands by his sides, watching every movement until she stood before him as naked as he was. Then he walked to her and set his hands on her until they were both moaning. When he backed them into the large shower, they both jumped at the cold water that streamed from the shower head. But as the water heated, so did their desires, and by the time the water was toasty, they were both gasping for air.

"How can you do this to me?" He lay his forehead on hers, closing his eyes. His arms were wrapped around her, holding tight. Her skin, slick and scented, pressed up against his.

She wanted him again, would always want him. "Mitch? Take me to bed." The shower was too small for them to do anything but touch each other. Not that it wasn't pleasant, but she needed him. All of him.

He looked into her eyes and shut off the water. Then he took his time drying her skin as she stood under the heat lamp in the bathroom. He kissed his way across her skin until she finally grabbed his hand and walked him into the next room.

The floor was cold, and they rushed across the hardwood until finally, they both jumped on the bed, laughing.

"I guess I could light a fire up here." He said.

"No, don't." She didn't want him to leave her side, so she ran her hands over every inch of him until their warmth heated the entire room.

"I want you so bad. Please, Mitch." He smiled down at her,

and she knew she'd already lost her heart as he slowly entered her. Their mixed groans were a sound she'd never forget. His smooth skin under her hands felt wonderful. His kisses branded her across every pore.

Knowing words would never be enough, she poured all her passion into each kiss until they were both on the verge. Then she pulled his head down to hers and looking him directly in the eyes, told him how she felt.

itch lay very still listening to his heartbeat settle. His eyes were closed as she ran her hands over his back, down to his butt. There would be marks there tomorrow where her nails had dug into his skin. He smiled.

He didn't know if he'd been hallucinating or not. He could have sworn that Sandi had said that she loved him. His smile disappeared. Pulling back, he looked down at her. Her hair was fanned out on the white sheets. Her dark skin glowed with the aftermath of their passions. He had never intended to let things go this far. How could he trust again after Suzanne? Then Sandi opened her eyes and he knew that he did trust her. He trusted her more than anyone else in his life. He could never imagine her betraying him, or anyone else in her life. It was rare in life to find people that honest and kindhearted. They just didn't come along very often. But with her, he could see that she would never do anything to hurt him. It just wasn't in her nature.

Leaning his head down to hers, he sighed. "I didn't mean for this to go this way. For us to follow this path." He pulled back and sat up. He wanted to see her face, to make sure that she understood his words. "We've only known each other for a couple weeks. I mean..." He ran his hands through his hair and he watched tears forming in her eyes. He dropped his hands and took her hands into his. "I can't believe that I can feel this much about you so quickly. It just doesn't happen. I don't know what we have, but I know I've never felt this way before."

She smiled at him and the fear in her eyes disappeared. "I feel the same way. I've known since the second I met you. I've known there was something about you. You stuck your neck out for someone halfway across the world, someone you'd never met. I'm so glad you did. I'm so lucky to have you. To be with you." She reached over and kissed him again.

"Sandi..." He kissed her and decided words couldn't express his thoughts. "How about I run downstairs and grab us a snack?"

She chuckled. "I could use a snack."

The next morning the sun was shining, and they hopped in the car with her paint supplies and headed out to find the little white church he'd known would be a perfect spot for her to paint.

The leaves weren't in full color, but a lot of them had turned overnight from the chill in the air. As they drove through the winding roads, her eyes were glued to the windows. They stopped at a small shop and had coffee and pastries. After another half-an-hour drive, they came across the small building set in the middle of a large green field. The trees that surrounded it were still very green, but he could just imagine the leaves in full fall colors.

She sat with a large sketch pad on her lap, since they hadn't found an easel anywhere. First, she sketched out the basic shapes.

"I'll probably wait until we get back to the house to paint

it, so I can prop this up somewhere." He sat next to her in the cool grass, watching every move, each line she created. It was like she'd captured every detail. It was amazing to him to see that her eyes picked up on all the angles. When he looked at the building, he noticed that it needed a good coat of paint and a few new shingles on the roof and small maintenance items that needed to be done. She pulled out the beauty in it all somehow. It took just over an hour for her to get the pencil outline complete. When they packed up, he decided to take a different route back to town. Less than ten minutes later, she was yelling at him to pull over. He stopped the car, worried something was wrong. When she jumped out and grabbed a large canvas she'd brought, he smiled as she rushed to the side of the road and started drawing the charming covered bridge he'd almost missed seeing. Apparently, there had been an old highway that went alongside the one they were on. The bridge looked like it hadn't been used in over a hundred years. Its charm was still intact. He leaned on the hood of the car and watched as she sat on the side of the highway, totally engrossed in her work. The sun was warm on his neck, and he realized he could enjoy driving around all day, watching her draw.

It took her a little over two hours to complete the drawing of the bridge. There were more angles and lines, and he watched as she included a lot of the trees and bushes that had grown up around the bridge. The water that flowed under it came alive in her drawing. He couldn't wait to see her add color to it all.

"Thanks for stopping. I've never seen a covered bridge before." She smiled as they drove back towards town. "I can't wait to paint these. I think I'll do the chapel in watercolors and the covered bridge in oils."

They drove up to the house, and Sandi eagerly got to work at the large dining table as he set out to make them some lunch. He was excited to see what she'd do with each canvas... By the time he carried in a bowl of homemade chicken soup and sourdough bread, she was already halfway done with the watercolor of the church.

"Wow, you're fast."

"On some things. Oils take longer, but I wanted to get this one done before I started on the bridge." She rubbed her hands together and he realized it was chilly in the room.

"I can start a fire in here." He started to get up.

"No, that's okay, the cold keeps me moving." They ate their soup, and she got back to work while he cleared the dishes. Then he jogged up the stairs and grabbed the pile of clothes that needed washing and straightened up the room they'd used. He found an old video of when he and Carter had visited last. He popped that into the machine and laughed as the pair of them took turns videoing each other water skiing. They had a few other buddies stay for a few nights and at one point there was a large party that flashed on the screen. He didn't know who had the camera, but when an image of Carter kissing Eve flashed on the screen, Mitchell was shocked. He didn't know they had ever been an item. He'd always thought they had hated each other the whole time. He'd have to make sure to razz his friends about the incident that had happened over a decade ago.

When he went back downstairs, she had set the water-color canvas aside and was tediously working on the oil color of the bridge. He could see why it took more time to work with the oils. She used smaller brushes and each stroke was controlled, where the watercolor brushstrokes were wild and more free-flowing. Here, the colors didn't blend. Instead, they ran along each other, highlighting the contrast and texture.

He stood over her for almost an hour watching her work. When the light started to dim in the room, he flipped on the lights overhead and moved a chair closer so he could watch her. They didn't speak. He didn't want to interrupt her, and no words were needed as she worked.

He was totally amazed at the piece when she finally started cleaning the brushes. He'd never seen anything more detailed or more beautiful.

"I've never seen anything more beautiful." He stood up as she leaned the canvas on the china hutch. They stood there looking at the canvas as his arm came around her shoulders. He realized everything felt right. She felt right in his arms. It felt good to have her there, to celebrate the beauty they had created together. He'd never expected something to just click, but being with her everything did, and he realized that he didn't know what the next step was.

IN THE NEXT FEW DAYS, they traveled all over the countryside. She went through almost three dozen canvases, filling them with the beautiful scenery they explored together. They had gone hiking a few times and had found a beautiful waterfall where they spent the day, her painting, him watching. They had packed a lunch and had ended up staying until almost dark.

The leaves were in full fall color now. Everything seemed to be so much more alive to her. They had made a run to a different art supply store a few towns away to get more supplies. Mitchell had even found a small portable easel that they could carry with them. She'd bought a small carry case for her paints, so she could paint on-site instead of having to go back to the house.

They spent the rainy days inside making love the entire day, and they spent the sunny days outside. Their evenings were filled with their passion for each other. He hadn't told her he loved her yet, and she was beginning to worry. She told him every chance she could without seeming too desperate.

It was on their second week there that he'd finally received a call from Ethan. When Mitchell got off the phone, his face was filled with concern.

"What? What is it?" She asked.

"That was Ethan. He was on assignment in Brazil. Apparently, the assignment went bad. He's finally back in the states and will check into your situation when he can. He told us to stay put for now and he'd send someone up here to help make sure everything is secure."

Part of her heart sank. She'd almost forgotten why they were hiding out. The last few days had seemed like a wonderful dream. Their time together was some of the best she'd ever had, and she didn't want it to end.

Now that Ethan was back, did that mean she would be going away? Starting a new life under some other name? In some other state, or worse, another country? She hadn't thought that far ahead. She couldn't imagine leaving Mitch. She knew he couldn't drop his life for her. He had too much to lose: his place, his business, his friendships, his family. He'd never leave it all for her. Especially since he still hadn't told her that he loved her yet. Why would he give everything up for her?

"Oh, I see." And for the first time in weeks, she did. This was just a short break for him. A reprieve from the mundane life. She didn't doubt that he cared for her. He showed her every time they made love. But he wasn't ready to commit to someone whose life was up in the air like hers was. "That's good." She tried to smile at him. The crease between his eyes increased and he began to frown. "Isn't it?"

"Yeah, it will be nice to know that your family won't be able to find you." He started pacing across the floor, still holding his phone. "Listen, I'm going to step out and make a few calls. I haven't checked in to the office for a few days."

"Sure," she got up and started to leave the room. "Mitch, I don't know what's going to happen to me in the future, but I hope that wherever I go, that we will still remember this time fondly." She smiled and then turned to walk out of the room.

She walked past the living room and went straight out the front door and out to the end of the long front porch. The American flag was still waving in the light breeze. She looked at it and thought of how different her life had been since she'd first come to this country. How much she had changed. Would she have recognized herself if she had looked into the future, five years ago?

Her clothes were all Americanized. She no longer wore the long hijabs demanded by her culture. She didn't paint her skin with henna, no longer wore the ornamental jewelry she'd grown to love as a little girl. For that matter, she no longer spoke in her native tongue or even had private thoughts in it either.

She leaned against the railing and watched the sailboats in the harbor. She loved this country for everything it stood for. Everything she'd ever desired. Freedom. She was hurt that some would never feel the freedom she had a taste of in the last five years. The thought of it disappearing scared her. She knew the penalty for what she'd done was death in her culture. Even though it wasn't condoned by the courts, that didn't mean it stopped it from happening. There had been several cases in the news the last few years where family members had tracked down girls here in America and Europe to inflict their punishments. She'd followed each story, wondering when it would be her turn. Living in fear. Thinking about it, she guessed she had never truly experienced freedom. At least not yet. Not until she was either dead or her family was.

She realized it came down to just that. Her or them. Pushing away from the railing, she started walking across the yard towards the pathway that led down to the water. When she made it to the beach, she was thankful for the cold breeze coming off the water. When it hit her face, she felt alive and realized that was what mattered the most.

No matter what her family did to her, they couldn't take her time with Mitchell away. She'd gladly give up her life today, knowing that she'd been truly happy once. Even if they were separated and she had to start a new life somewhere else, she would always remember this time as the happiest in her life.

She made the decision to enjoy the next few days at least until Ethan made his move to step in and move her. She would do everything in her power to make this time truly enjoyable.

"There you are." She spun around and saw Mitchell walking fast towards her, worry in his eyes. "I've been looking everywhere for you."

"Oh, I'm sorry. I decided to go for a short walk." She looked around and realized she was farther from the house than she realized. When he approached he took her in a gentle hug.

"Here." He removed his jacket. "You're freezing." He helped her put it on and, she realized she was cold. She'd been so deep in thought she hadn't known how cold it was. The wind had picked up, and she shivered as it tossed her hair around her face.

"Let's head back?" She nodded and smiled at him.

"Is everything okay in the city?" She asked.

"Yeah, so far so good. I've told them I'll be away for a few more days." He was frowning again, and she wished more than anything that he would open up to her and give her a glimpse into what his thoughts were. She'd never been in a relationship before and didn't know the etiquette of how to ask him to open up to her.

They walked back to the house, hand in hand, in silence. For the rest of the evening, he was quiet. After dinner, she walked into her temporary studio. It was one of the larger bedrooms on the second floor that had a large desk where she could paint. She sat down and started working on another piece. However, after a few minutes, she set her brush down. She didn't feel like painting anymore that evening.

The sun was setting and the colors in the room were vibrant on the white walls. She went and laid down on the small bed and watched the shadows float across the ceiling and the walls.

Memories flashed, and the shadows became images in front of her eyes. Faces of people she once knew, places she'd been, appeared on the blank walls, the colors adding to the calmness of her thoughts. Then a large shadow loomed over her, dark eyes resting on her, boring into her, causing her to cringe in pain. Her hands and face were slashed open with rocks as everyone she'd ever loved threw stone after stone at her as she knelt in a dark pit.

Then it all stopped, and one shadow stepped forward. Pointing at her with a long thin finger, a deep voice cried, "ṭraikṭara, ṭraikṭara." Over and over he called her a traitor.

Then he lifted his other hand and in it, he held a long sharp blade. Just as it arched down, she called out, "No, Pita!" and sat up.

CHAPTER 16

"Shh, it's okay. It was just a bad dream." Mitch sat next to her on the small bed, holding her still as she cried into his shoulder. He ran her hair through his fingers and realized he never wanted to let her go.

Ever since the call from Ethan, his mind had been consumed with trying to figure out how to get her to stay. He knew there was no way they could possibly live in constant fear of her family. After all, Ethan had confirmed the worse. Her father and cousin had enough power that they were in the states under diplomatic immunity. Meaning they could do whatever they wanted, go wherever they wanted, and most importantly, stay as long as they needed.

Ethan was going to have his men check into it further. If he could prove they were abusing it or had committed a crime, they could be sent back home. Until then, they were free to come and go. The police were limited as to what they could do; which is why after the taxi incident, they'd never heard from them again.

She leaned on his shoulder now crying, and he closed his eyes, enjoying the feel and smell of her. Would he miss this when she was gone? Gone somewhere, hiding for the rest of her life. He didn't want to think about her having a new life. Maybe falling for someone else, marrying, and maybe even raising children.

"I'm sorry. I guess the dream affected me more than usual," she said, leaning back and wiping the tears from her face.

"More so than usual? How often do you have them?" Since their arrival, he'd noticed a few times where she'd been twitching at night, but he had always been there to pull her into his arms, away from the dreams.

She shrugged her shoulders. "More often since I know they are close."

He ran his hands down the side of her face, brushing back a strand of dark hair back. She had dark circles under her eyes and he noticed a lost look in the dark pools that hadn't been there before.

"Ethan and I are going to make sure they never find you." He leaned down and placed a soft kiss on her lips. "Come on, I've made some dinner and found Caddyshack. You've never experienced comedy until you've experienced Chevy Chase in Caddyshack." He smiled, trying to lighten the mood.

The next day it rained and instead of staying in the room with her, watching her paint, Mitch used his phone as a computer and did a little more research. Diplomatic immunity laws were long and so in depth, he was getting a headache trying to understand the basics. Just the fact that her family would have gone through such trouble to get their government's approval to come to the States under this law told him the lengths they would go to get their hands on her.

He felt hopeless as he walked up the stairs. Just as he reached the landing, his phone rang. When he walked into the room, he felt even more hopeless.

Sitting beside her, he waited until her attention was off the painting and on him.

"I have to go into the city tonight. I shouldn't be long, but something major has come up. I'll be back here by tomorrow evening. Will you be okay by yourself for a night?"

He saw the worry in her eyes. "Sure. I'll be fine. There are plenty of supplies, and I was going to try and finish this piece anyway." She smiled.

He looked at the painting of the beach scene and saw the outline of a couple walking hand in hand. His hope for the future was very strong. He wanted nothing more than to walk with her along the beach hand-in-hand for the rest of his life.

"I can stay." He watched her face.

"No," she shook her head. "Your work is important. I understand. You've been gone almost three weeks. Go." She smiled and squeezed his hand. "I'll be okay. There's no way my family knows where I am. Besides, Ethan's man is supposed to be here later tomorrow." He could see her smile falter.

"I'll try to be back around noon. Is there anything from my place you need?" He asked.

She thought about it. "No, I'm fine. Just hurry back." She leaned over and kissed him softly, causing him to want to stay longer.

Ten minutes later, he was in the car driving out of town, Sandi on his mind. He'd never really felt this way about anyone before. He knew he trusted her more than he'd ever trusted anyone before. She had even trumped Carter, his best friend from grade school. How he'd ever allowed their relationship to move to this level was beyond him. She was everything to him. Driving along the highway, he realized he even missed her in the car as he drove.

Sitting in silence was different with her in the car. The

silence seemed less ... quiet. Maybe it was her scent that he missed? The soft feminine smell seemed to follow her everywhere. He didn't think he could describe it if he had to. All he knew was that when it was gone, he missed it. It was there in her hair, on her skin. This got him thinking about the softness of her and how he'd always enjoyed finding another soft spot to explore on her.

She was everything he'd ever dreamed of, everything he'd ever hoped of having. Then why was he having such a hard time saying those simple words to her? He'd said them to plenty of women before. He'd told Suzanne he'd loved her before she'd even said the words herself.

Maybe it was because it hadn't meant the same as it did now? When he said it this time he knew, somehow, that she would be the last woman he'd ever say it to.

Just then his phone rang. Switching it to speaker he answered the phone.

"Hey buddy, how's hiding out going?" Carter's voice sounded in his speakers.

"Good, I'm on the road and should be there in a few hours," he said, watching a truck pass him.

"Here?" Carter asked.

"Yeah, I got the message that the Travis account was going sour and you guys needed me to come in and smooth things over." Mitch glanced in the rearview mirror.

"What? The Travis account is going south? Why am I the last to hear about this?" Mitch could hear Carter talking to someone. He presumed it was Eve.

"Uh, hey buddy, I don't know where you got your intel, but the Travis account is secure. Eve's on the phone with them now and everything looks fine."

Mitchell thought about it, then slammed on his brakes and spun the car around. "Shit! Listen, I've gotta go." He hung up the phone and punched the gas. He was almost twenty minutes out of town and prayed he was fast enough.

By the time he arrived back at the house, the sun was setting and the first thing he noticed was how dark the house was. He jumped from the car before it had fully stopped. Leaving the door open, he rushed towards the back door of the house, only to find it kicked in, its glass broken, shattered all over the floor.

He rushed in fear causing everything to feel slowed down. Flipping on the lights, he screamed her name over and over. Running through the house, he searched every room and found nothing. The room she had used as a studio was thrashed, paint supplies thrown everywhere. When he rushed in, he'd thought the red paint on the floor was blood and his heart stopped. Then he noticed the tube of oil paint, squashed as if stepped on by a boot. He followed the red bootprint into the hallway, back down the stairs and out the open front door.

He ran into the kitchen and grabbed the flashlight, then ran back out the door. He headed towards the beach at a sprint.

Where would she go? Was he going to be too late? He stood there listening and after a minute he heard a gunshot and then a scream. Running towards the cliffs he ran faster then he'd ever run in his life, praying the entire way.

SANDI WATCHED Mitch's car disappear around the twisted drive. She stood there for a while thinking about their relationship. She didn't know much about how to show him what she felt. She'd tried telling him, but it seemed her words just weren't enough.

She leaned her head against the window and felt like

crying. Instead, she stood up and walked back over to her desk. She knew that engrossing herself in her art would help the time alone pass. She was so engrossed in her art; she didn't register the noise downstairs at first.

When the sounds of glass breaking finally did register, she panicked. Looking around for a weapon, the only thing that was handy was her paints. She stood against the back of the door, barely breathing as she listened for any sounds.

They'd been in the house for several weeks now, and she knew every sound associated with going up and down the stairs and hallway. When she heard the sound of the floorboards on the stairs, she held her breath.

Questions flooded her mind. How was she going to escape? Where would she go? She didn't have a car or a phone. She didn't even know where the nearest neighbor's house was. When she heard the door upstairs open, she bolted from the room and ran down the stairs. She shot out the front door and ran across the yard without looking back.

When she hit the tree line, she slowed down and looked back at the house. She saw a shadow in the window of her art room, then it was gone, and she knew he was coming after her. She turned and ran for her life.

When she heard footsteps behind her, she ran faster. She thought she was on a pathway, but when it opened up, she realized she'd run right towards the lighthouse at the end of the cove. As she stopped in the clearing, she got her first glimpse of the large white building. Large rocks jutted all around it. It sat, a large white beacon in the dying light. She made her way over the rocks carefully, heading away from the building, not knowing if there was any way to escape. She knew the lighthouse was at the tip of the cove. She'd meant to head the other way and in her panicked state, she'd gone the wrong direction. Stupid, she scolded herself. Just like the dumb women in those horror movies she hated watching. She slowly made her way over the dark rocks and when she hit the grass, she sprinted. She thought she'd actually lost her pursuer, but she stopped short when a shadow appeared before her.

She screamed and skidded to a stop, landing on her hip and hands in the small rock pathway. Pebbles embedded in her palms and ripped the jeans she wore. When she finally stopped she looked up into her father's face.

"Pita?" She held her breath, not knowing what to do. He stood over her, like so many of her nightmares from the last five years.

"Palatu." He wore all black. Gone was his dhoti and long robes. In their place, he wore black jeans, tennis shoes, and a leather jacket and gloves. She'd never seen her father dressed in American clothes, and she stared at him like he was a stranger.

"Palatu, why are you running away from me?" The sound of her native tongue was like ice on her soul.

She quickly stood up and rubbed her hands against her jeans, not realizing that her blood smeared across the front of her legs.

"You're here to punish me for leaving home." She said, holding her chin up high.

He nodded. "But why do you run?"

She stood tall. "I don't want to die. I'm happy here. I've created a good life. I work hard. I make my own way and I've found love."

"I know; I've been watching you. Is he good to you?" Her father asked.

She felt herself shaking but tried to control most of it by holding her hands together in front of her. "Yes, he's a good man. I wish more than anything to wed him and have many children."

He nodded. "I've seen you two together. I think he takes

good care of you."

She was confused. Had he been watching them? How long?

"Palatu, I've only come to see you are happy. If you were not happy, I was going to take you back home. To your mother. She worries so." Her father's voice deepened a little.

She looked at him and in the dying light, she couldn't quite read his face. Was this a trap? Why was he talking like he was trying to help her?

"I don't understand. What about Anish?" She looked behind her.

"Anish? He is here." Her father asked, his eyes looking around.

She was more confused than before.

"Anish, he said he was here to take my money, that the family had suffered because I left. That I had to be punished because I left you with nothing."

Her father stood still and finally, as the clouds disappeared for a moment and the full light of the stars and the moon hit him, she saw his face for the first time. He looked older. His black hair was streaked with silver and looked thinner on the top. She noticed wrinkles around his eyes and mouth. He looked tired. "Anish has talked to you?" He asked.

She nodded. "He threatened me. He hurt someone close to Mitchell. He broke into my apartment and broke everything."

"Anish did this?" His voice was growing louder.

"I thought you had helped him." She took a step closer to him as she saw the sadness come into his eyes.

"No, I knew of nothing. I've been following you. Trying to decide if you were happy. We came here together, but shortly after we found where you lived, he took off. I followed you here and have been here since you arrived." He said, looking into her eyes.

She thought about it. "You aren't mad at me? You aren't here to kill me?"

"No, my pet. I could never hurt you. Your mother and I, we only want to know if you are happy. When you left, you took our heart. We realize we were wrong, trying to force you to marry Ishat. We didn't know he requested the mādā janānga vikrti until the day after you were gone. We would have never let him harm you."

Her heart mended the rip that had been torn for so long. Realizing all the years she'd believed that her parents didn't care had caused the guilt to sink in.

Just then they both turned as another voice chimed in. "Finally." Anish stood next to a tree breathing hard. "Good, you're both here. It's easier to take care of things this way. I've waited for a long time to get the two of you together. Ever since my father was imprisoned I've thought about my revenge."

Sandi realized he had a gun in his hand when the moonlight reflected off its barrel. She gasped and took a step back towards her father.

Anish continued talking and walking slowly towards them. "You, Haidar, I'm going to kill you for sending my father here in the first place. You only thought of Sannidhi. She was just a stupid girl. Yet you sent your brother across the world and look at where it got him. Life in prison like a common thief."

Sandi tried to think. If she ran, she knew Anish would shoot her. Then there was her father. She didn't know how fast he could run, but after having Anish chase her through the streets of Manhattan, she knew she would have a hard time staying in front of him. She wished Mitchell was here.

"Sannidhi, I'm going to enjoy killing you. I think I will seek vengeance first. Take my time and enjoy it. I've always had a thing for you, you know. Besides, what good are you for? You've caused my family nothing but pain. Everything I have was taken when my father was incarcerated."

Her heart stopped as she realized how evil her cousin was. Her father pulled her back another step, holding her still in case she tried to run. She knew he thought the same thing, that neither of them would make it very far.

"Anish put the gun down. This is not how you deal with your family. I'm the head of the family. I'll take care of my daughter myself." Her father stepped forward, putting his body next to hers. They stood shoulder to shoulder.

She heard it then. Mitchell's voice screaming her name over and over again. Her cousin heard it, too. He swung his arm and head towards the house and then he spun back around and pointed the gun at her chest. Just before he squeezed the trigger, she was pushed aside by her father.

She screamed as she felt her father's body jerk and land next to her on the rocky ground. When she looked up again, her cousin stood over her, a twisted smile on his face.

"I'm going to kill your man when he gets here. I'll make you watch as his body is drained of life, then I'll take you next to his cold body. I'll slit your throat and have your family's money to line my wallet."

Just then Mitchell ran into the clearing. When he saw Anish standing over her, he growled as he sprinted towards them. Her cousin turned, starting to aim the gun at Mitchell. She viewed it all as it was a movie in slow motion. Fear closed her throat so that she couldn't even scream.

Using all her strength, she kicked out and landed a blow on her cousin's legs. Anish fell forward just as the gun went off. Grabbing hold of him, she rolled with a kick, taking her and her cousin towards the edge of the cliff. Not knowing where the gun was, she continued the motion until she heard Mitchell scream her name, but she didn't stop until she felt her body start to fall.

CHAPTER 17

"I've got you." Mitch was gripping Sandi's arm, praying for the strength to hold on. His side stung where the bullet had grazed him, but he wouldn't let go. Couldn't let go.

As he looked down, he saw her cousin's body twisted at the bottom of the small cliff, his neck at an odd angle. Focusing his eyes on Sandi's face, he started pulling her up towards him. She kicked her feet, trying to dig into the mud and rocks, dislodging them as she tried to pull herself up. Finally, when she was back on solid ground, he pulled her close and held on for a moment.

Then she was pushing him away and running to her father's side.

"No! Pita." She knelt over him, tears falling from her face. She said something else to him in Hindi and Mitch noticed the blood pooling around the man's chest.

"Mitch? Help me." She looked up into his eyes and he would have done anything for her.

Kneeling beside the man, he took off his jacket and placed

it over the hole in his chest. Applying pressure. He pulled his cell phone from his pocket and dialed 911.

"Pita! I don't know what to do. Please stay with me." Sandi begged. "Don't go." She cried seeing her father's face go ashen. She knew he was beyond help. There was something in his eyes that told her he was ready to go.

"Palatu, Sannidhi, my daughter, my light. I'm sorry I caused you such fear. I never meant to hurt you. Can you understand this? I only wished to see you happy. When I was younger, I was blinded by my brother and the desire of money. He talked me into binding you with Ishat's family because they had money and power. But what he started, I couldn't stop. When my brother shamed our family, I knew then that I had to find you. To make things right with you. I saw your painting in Bhubaneswar. I knew it was yours. It took me months to find the dealer. When I came here, I did everything to find you. I never meant to scare you." His hand came up and cupped her face. "Never to scare you my pet. I love you, my daughter."

The tears fell from her face as his hand went limp in hers and then dropped from her face.

Mitch watched the scene, and his heart broke a little as Sandi cried over her father's lifeless body. He stood there, not sure what to do, not exactly sure what had happened.

He knew the pain of losing family, but there were no words he could say to take some of it away. Instead, he knelt there, looking down at the scene, wishing that her freedom hadn't cost her so much.

By the time the police arrived, Sandi and Mitch were standing in the driveway, Sandi silently crying on Mitch's shoulder. She stayed back at the house with a female officer as he walked the police out to the scene. Four officers followed him, asking him questions as they went. His jacket still lay over her father's face. The gun was still by her cousin's body at the bottom of the cliff.

Once he'd shown them the bodies and described what he'd seen, an older office walked with him back to the house. They were asked the same questions over and over. A medic had patched the small scratch where the bullet had passed by his ribs. It stung a little but was quickly forgotten. An hour later, he made a pot of coffee, passing out cups to all the officers still on the scene. It seemed every police officer in the small town was at the house now.

When the coroner's van came, he tried to keep Sandi from noticing as they carted the bodies past the front of the house. The female officer was a big help in keeping her occupied. She asked questions about Sandi's paintings and tried to keep Sandi's mind from what was happening outside.

Several officers helped him put a wood plank over the broken glass, closing up the back window in the door until it could be replaced. He called Carter and explained everything, His friend was glad that they were okay and told him not to worry about the door, that he'd have it replaced later that week.

Finally, hours later, when everyone had left, they walked upstairs. It felt like his body was at past exhaustion. He imagined that she felt the same way.

Walking into the bathroom he started the bathwater, making sure to add some of the bath salts he'd bought her from a local shop. Then he walked into the next room and when he saw her sitting on the edge of the bed, looking down at her hands, he pulled her to her feet. Her eyes were dull and red-rimmed from all the crying. Her face was a little pale and her hair was a tangled mess. He wanted to gather her up and kiss away the pain.

"I thought...I thought he..." She started to sniffle.

"Shh, I know. We both did. I've drawn you a bath. Come on, I'd like to clean these cuts on your hands."

She looked down, and he could tell she'd long forgotten about the small pebbles embedded into her skin. She nodded her head and when they entered the bathroom, he helped her undress, taking care when he noticed her knees were also cut.

When she stepped into the tub, steam rose from the water and she hissed at the warmth.

"Too hot?" He asked.

"No, it's fine." She sank into the water, and he watched as she ducked her head under. She ran her hands through her hair, scrubbing her scalp before surfacing.

He walked over to the cabinets, looking for something to help clean her palms. Finding a new pair of tweezers, he grabbed a small container of Neosporin from the shelf and a small hand towel off the rack. He moved a stool beside the bathtub and gently took her hand.

"Relax. I'll try to be as gentle as I can." He set to work, removing the small rocks from her skin. By the time he was done with one hand, she looked completely relaxed floating in the water. Her hair was fanned out around her face and her eyes were closed. Since her other hand was across her body, she had to sit up as he worked on her left palm.

"I'm sorry about your dad. I didn't understand everything he said near the end, but from what I could gather he didn't mean you any harm?"

"No, he came here to make sure I was happy. Only to see if I was happy." Her voice hitched, and she closed her eyes on the pain.

"I'm sorry." The realization that her father had not been the evil person he'd assumed made him feel even worse.

"He saved me. He stepped in front of the bullet. If it wasn't for him..." She started.

"Shh." He gathered her up in a light hug, getting his shirt wet and not caring.

"Mitch, I'm getting you wet," she said a few seconds later.

"I don't care. All that matters is that you're safe. I don't know what I would have done." He shook his head, stopping himself. "Here." He stood and grabbed a towel, holding it up for her to walk into.

They walked into the bedroom. "Are you hungry?" When she shook her head no, he walked over to the window and stood, looking out at the darkness.

"I meant to tell you sooner." He turned back towards her. She sat with her hair dripping wet, holding the towel closed with her hands clenched to her chest.

He walked over and knelt before her. "Sannidhi Rangan, I love you more than life itself. I don't know what I would do without you. I've never trusted someone as much as I trust you with these words, with my heart. I love you."

She lifted her hand and touched his face.

"I love you, too, Mitchell Kovich. I've loved you since the first time I saw you over five years ago. I've dreamed of being with you, of starting a life with you, since that first night."

She smiled down at him. "I could never imagine my life without you."

He smiled up at her. "You will never have to."

THE NEXT MORNING, they spent a good deal of time cleaning the house, preparing to leave. Sandi had insisted that they leave it cleaner than when they had arrived. His fingers and back said he'd worked hard enough to get it there, and the place seemed to shine. Sandi had packed up all their new items in bags. It took several trips to get all her artwork out to the car. The canvases filled the entire back seat.

"I hope we can come here again. I think I could spend my whole life here and not feel like I've captured the beauty completely." She sighed, looking around.

He pulled her close and kissed her, enjoying the feel of her melting into his arms. Just then his cell phone rang.

Looking at the number, he stepped away and answered. Five minutes later he walked back over to her.

"The authorities are sending your father and cousin's bodies back home for burial. Since they were here under diplomatic immunity, there is a huge pile of paperwork and legal tape they have to go through. But they think they have enough from us. They just wanted to let us know that we're clear to head back home." He smiled. "I guess since we have their permission, we can leave now."

She nodded. "Mitchell, I'd like to go back and visit my mother. Maybe help her bury my father."

He smiled and pulled her close. "I think a trip to India is just what we need. I'll arrange everything when we get back."

She looked up at him and smiled. "For the first time in my life, I'm looking forward to going home."

The car ride back to the city seemed to go faster than the trip up to Maine had. The leaves had all fallen and when they reached Boston, a light dusting of snow was actually falling.

As she listened to the wipers cleaning the flakes from the windshield, she imagined what life would be like a year from now. They hadn't talked about marriage but knew that was the path she wanted to take with him. Looking over at him as he drove, she smiled and thought about what their children would look like and wondered how many they would have.

"Four." She said out loud, shocking herself. He turned and looked at her and she blushed, turning her head towards the window.

"Four what?" He asked, smiling.

"Nothing." She laughed nervously.

"Oh, no. You don't get to play that game. Come on. Spill. Four what?" He took her hand.

She turned back to him. "Fine, I was thinking about our future. Do you want kids?"

He choked a little. "Well," he said recovering. "Sure. I haven't really thought about it." He tilted his head and stole glances at her as he drove. "Four, huh?"

She nodded her head, biting her bottom lip.

"I could do four." He smiled at her. "I guess we're going to need a bigger place, though. Maybe someplace away from the city."

"That would be wonderful." She sighed.

"We'd need at least five bedrooms, plus an office and a larger studio for your art." He was thinking now. She could see his eyebrows crinkle. "Someplace by the water. I never did get to take you out on the water this time. Plus, I've been thinking, since it's just your mother back home, how would you feel about bringing her back with us? I could see about getting her a green card. I know someone with connections." He smiled.

Sandi realized that if she hadn't already given him her heart, he would have stolen it, just then. Tears came to her eyes and she nodded her head.

MITCHELL'S PHONE rang shortly after they arrived back at his place. When he saw the name, he immediately answered it.

"What?" He was shocked. "What do you mean he's been shot?"

Sandi walked over to him and held onto his arm, looking at his face for answers. Mitchell's body began to shake.

"How bad?" He shook his head. "No, we can be there soon." He hung up. "That was Ric. Ethan's been shot. He was protecting a senator's daughter, the one he was with in Brazil. I guess something went wrong and he's been shot. He's in a hospital in Austin."

"Let's go. We're already packed." She looked up at him. "After all, we both owe him so much.

It took him a while on the phone to set everything up, but finally, an hour after arriving, they were in a cab on the way to the airport. Images of his friend, injured, flashed through his mind. Maybe it was everything that had happened in the last few weeks finally catching up with him, but he felt weary.

Then Sandi reached over and took his hand in hers. He traced the small bandages that covered the wounds on her palms and when she smiled at him, he knew everything was going to be okay.

When they arrived at the hospital in Austin the next day, Ethan was propped up on the bed smiling across the room at a dark-haired woman who looked very annoyed.

"Mitchell! Sandi! Come on in. Welcome to the party." He shook Mitchell's hand. Sandi smiled as she walked over and placed a soft kiss on his cheek.

"You're okay?" she asked.

"This?" He nodded to the bandages over his chest. "Oh, it's nothing. I've had worse."

"So he keeps saying," the woman in the corner said, walking over to them. "I'm Ann Rhodes."

Sandi and Mitch shook her hand.

"How's it going with you two? Did you find out anything about your dad?" Ethan asked Sandi.

An hour later, after they had caught Ethan and Ann up on her family matters, they stood around ready to leave.

"You don't have to rush off," Ethan said, holding Ann's hand.

"We're heading to India. We found Sandi's passport and

our flight leaves in a few hours anyway. Sandi wanted to be there to help bury her father. You know, be there for her mother."

Ethan nodded his head. "Thanks for coming over to check up on me. As you can see, I'm on the mend." He smiled up at Ann.

Sandi stood there holding Mitchell's hand as a couple walked into the room. The woman was small with long dark hair, the man tall and blond and holding a wiggling little girl.

"Ethan?" The woman walked over and hugged Ethan lightly.

"Rob, Ric. There's my Rose," Ethan said when the little girl held her arms out. "Sorry, baby, I think daddy better hold onto you for now." Then Ethan turned and smiled. "Sandi, this is my sister Roberta and my brother-in-law, Ric Derby. They got here earlier today."

Sandi stood there and realized she was finally meeting the last man who had risked everything for her freedom. Looking at the woman, she knew that Roberta was the cop her uncle, Anish's father, had shot, five years ago.

"I'm sorry." The words escaped her mouth as she shook Ric's hand. He laughed, and Roberta smiled.

"You have nothing to be sorry about." He pulled his wife into his arm. "If things hadn't gone the way they had, I would have never met the woman I love, and we wouldn't have this little beauty." He kissed his daughter's cheek.

Sandi smiled as Mitch stepped forward and shook his friend's hand. "Ric, it's good to see you."

"You, too. I hear you've had some excitement the last few weeks." Ric handed his daughter off to Roberta who walked over and sat next to Ethan.

Mitchell laughed and pulled Sandi to his side. "Like you said, nothing that wasn't worth the outcome.

Sandi stood on the shore and looked out across the calm waters. She'd never imagined she'd be so happy. Her supplies were back at her studio since today was not for painting. Instead, she stood there watching the water lap at the sand, and when Mitchell walked up behind her, wrapping his arms around her, she smiled.

"Well? What do you think?" He pulled her around, so she looked up at him.

Stepping back, Sandi scanned the shore. Large dark rocks lined the little beach. Tall hills rolled with grass that swayed in the warm breeze. She could imagine the scene in every season and knew that she could easily paint it all. Then she looked up towards the large house and could just make out the second-floor balcony and the green roof of the massive place. It was a bigger town just down the shore from Carter's place, but it would do nicely.

"It's perfect. I can imagine raising our children here, painting here." She turned to Mitchell again. "Living here with you for the rest of our lives."

"Then it's settled. It's ours." He smiled down at her.

"There is one last bit of business we've yet to discuss." He pulled out a small box from his jacket.

She held her breath as he opened the box, and she looked down at the large emerald ring.

"It matches your eyes." She smiled as she took the ring between her fingers.

"Is that a yes?" He smiled.

"You've known my answer for over a year." She smiled at him. "Yes, I'll marry you. I'll live in this beautiful house with you, raise four children, and live happily ever after." He laughed and spun her around, kissing her until they were both breathless.

IF YOU'VE ENJOYED this book, please consider leaving a review where you purchased it. Thanks! --Jill

PROLOGUE

Carter watched Eve from across the room. For the last ten years of his life, he'd watched her every chance he could. He would consider himself a borderline stalker if she wasn't one of his best friends. He didn't know if she knew that he watched her or if she knew how he felt, but he wasn't ready to risk it. Yet.

A few hours later, however, he'd had the right mix of lack of food, too much sun, and too much beer. When he'd walked into his grandparents' old place, he'd accidentally bumped into her in the upstairs hallway. He hadn't even known she was in the house. He'd thought she was still outside with the many other guests, either on the dock soaking up the sun, or out on the boat, water skiing. But there she was, just outside his grandparents' old bedroom. Instincts had kicked in and before he knew it, he'd pushed her through the door, shutting it with his foot as he'd swooped in for the most fantastic kiss he'd ever had. She'd tasted like strawberries and felt smoother than silk as he'd run his hands over her half-naked body. For a split second, he thought she'd arched into him and relaxed into the kiss. But then they had heard a cough and a click, then jumped apart like they'd been caught kissing, and well, they had. By one of Eve's best friends, Susan.

For the next week, Carter hadn't known how to approach her. Or what to say. Did he say anything? Or act like nothing had happened.

When he had finally approached her, she'd looked at her feet and told him she was getting married to her longtime boyfriend, Steve. His heart had been broken. That night he'd gone out with Mitch, his other best friend, and over their second pitcher of beer, they'd come up with a business plan that had rocketed them to the big times.

The next years of his life were a blur. He and Mitch spent all their time building their ad agency, Kovich & Edwards Agency, into a multimillion-dollar business. He'd stayed focused and every time he'd seen Eve, he'd tried not to think about that perfect kiss one hot summer day in Maine.

But when Carter had walked into his office a few years later to see Eve crying and sitting next to Mitch, he'd realized he had one more chance at happiness.

"I caught Steve cheating on me," she blurted out and he could see she was on the verge of tears.

"Carter, I've just saved our butts. I hired Eve to take over the Johnson contract. Actually, she's going to be taking half your clients, so you can have some more time in the office to straighten out the mess." Mitch smiled at Eve and patted her hand as she sniffled into a Kleenex.

"What?" Carter just stood there, and if his mind hadn't been so focused on how beautiful Eve was, even red-eyed, he probably could have pieced together what his friend was saying.

"You don't have to hire me," Eve said as she wiped her eyes.

Carter's mind jumped into gear. Eve was single. For the first time in almost eight years, she was single again. There was no way he was going to let this opportunity slip by him again.

He slowly walked over and sat across from her, really taking in how she looked. He could no longer see her red swollen eyes, but only how she'd looked that day in his grandparents' bedroom: wet, half-naked, and in his arms. Not to mention the feel of her skin under his hands or the taste of her lips. "No, it's fine. Welcome aboard." He smiled and knew it was going to be the hardest thing in the world working with the woman he desired so much.

CHAPTER 1

She could hear talking, but every time she tried to focus, she would slip back into the darkness. One voice stood out, however; it was constantly there. Its richness warmed her. She felt hands on her, cold hands. They came and went, lifting her, moving her, but she didn't respond. It was almost as if her mind was locked in a room, unable to respond to anything.

Finally, it was quiet, and she slept. Then there was a bright light and she squinted as she raised her arms up to shield her eyes from the light.

"Eve?" The deep voice said just above her.

"Eve?" She opened her eyes and saw a dark-haired man leaning over her. She blinked a few times, trying to get his face into better focus. Her eyes refused to focus at first; she looked up at him as if seeing him through a haze. Finally, he came into focus and she noticed his chocolate eyes hovered just above hers. There was a thick covering of stubble on his chin, and it was obvious that he hadn't shaved in a while. She ran her eyes slowly over the nice shape of his jaw and wondered how it would feel if she reached up and ran her fingers over it. His hair was messed up like he'd run his hands through it. Would it be as soft as it looked? His shirt buttons were opened, and she saw dried blood spots around the neck.

She went to move, to try and wipe her eyes. "No, sweetie," he said in the rich voice she'd come to know. "Don't move. Your wrist is sprained." He held her other hand and for the first time, she noticed a dull pain radiating from her left wrist.

Someone else spoke from across the room. He looked up, away from her, to answer them. When he looked back down at her, he smiled. "Mitchell and Sandi are here. Sandi's going to go find a doctor." She watched a tear slip down his cheek. Raising her good hand, she wiped it from his face. The wetness on her fingertips felt warm.

"Hey there." Another head leaned over her. This one was blonde, and the man had sea green eyes. He too looked like he could use a shave. The worry in both their eyes matched.

"I…" Her throat felt sore. She cleared it and tried to talk again, but just as she opened her mouth this time, the doctor walked in.

"Hi, good morning. I hear our patient is up."

"Yes," the men said in unison.

"Good." An older, gray-haired man leaned over her now. His face was wrinkled, and he had kind, blue eyes. "How are you feeling? Mrs. Taylor?"

She blinked a few times and fear crept into her mind. "I… Where am I?" She didn't know what to say. She had so many questions, but this one seemed to be the most important at the moment.

"You're at University Hospital in Chicago." Then the older man looked up, away from her. "If you don't mind, I'd like to examine her. Maybe you can run downstairs for a cup of coffee?" She heard people leaving the room and the click of the door being shut.

A young, blonde nurse leaned over her now. "Here, would you like to sit up?" The bed began moving and soon she was looking at a small, empty hospital room. She could see her feet tucked under a large green blanket. She wiggled her toes and saw the blanket move.

"Good. I see you moving your feet." The nurse smiled at her.

"Can you tell me, what's the last thing you remember?" The doctor flashed a light at her face and her head exploded. She shut her eyes and grabbed her head with her good hand. Pain spread from her left temple down her jaw, through her neck, and into her entire body.

"I'm sorry, dear. I know your eyes are sensitive to the light, but I have to check your pupils. Can you open your eyes for me?"

She shook her head slightly. The pain was almost too much to bear.

"Okay, we can try again later. Can you tell me how many fingers I'm holding up?" She slowly opened her eyes and looked. It was blurry, but she could see three fingers.

"Three."

"Good. How's your vision? Can you see the clock on the wall there?" He pointed across the room. She could just make out a dark circle but wouldn't have known it was a clock. She shook her head.

"Okay, that's okay. Sometimes a bump on the head like the one you took will play havoc with your sight. It may take a few days until everything is back in focus." She watched him write something down. "Can you tell me the last thing you remember?"

She thought about it. The last thing she remembered. Everything was blurry. She was in a hospital room in

Chicago. There was a dark-haired man whose voice was familiar to her, a blond man named Mitchell, and someone named Sandi. Looking up at the doctor, she shook her head, no.

"No? No, you can't tell me what happened? Or no, you don't remember what happened to you?"

"I don't remember anything." She felt the bedspread under her fingers and gripped the cotton. She felt short of breath and found it difficult to swallow. "I can't remember anything. Who I am. Who those people were. Why I'm in Chicago. I can't even remember what I look like or my name."

Two days earlier

Eve couldn't believe her eyes. For the millionth time in her life, Carter Edwards was on her nerves. She watched him sprint towards her with a small black bag in hand, his usual smile pasted on his face. Most women would swoon over his dashing personality and rugged good looks. She, however, found it hard not to grind her teeth in frustration.

"Good," he said as he stopped right in front of her. "I made it." He stowed his bag in the overhead compartment and sat next to her in the aisle seat. Instantly the large plane felt smaller.

"What are you doing here?" She tried not to talk between clenched teeth. Relaxing her jaw, she took a deep breath as she waited for him to answer her.

"There, all ready." He nodded to the flight attendant who blushed a little and turned to start her pre-flight tasks. "I decided to join you in Chicago. Tom Russell can be quite overbearing. I thought I'd tag along to help out."

He leaned back in his seat and crossed his long legs, looking rather comfortable in such a small space. She knew exactly how to handle Tom Russell—the same way she handled all her other clients and, on occasion, her boss. She squinted at him and wished he would just go away.

"How did you get the seat next to mine? This flight was booked." She looked around.

He smiled and looked at her. "I have my ways. Aww, now, don't give me that look. You won't even know I'm here."

How could she not know he was there? He seemed to suck up all the air in the compartment and she swore the walls of the plane had just moved in three feet.

She tried to relax, knowing it was going to be a long flight and trip. A few hours sitting next to Carter seemed like nothing compared to four days in Chicago with him. As the plane started to taxi, she tried not to think about how close his knee was to hers.

For years, she'd tried not to think about Carter in that way. Even when she'd been engaged to that lying, cheating… No—she interrupted her thoughts. Negative thoughts produced negative actions. She started doing her breathing exercises.

"Thinking about the scum ball again?" She heard the humor in Carter's voice and tried not to lash out at him.

"It's really none of your concern." She leaned her head back and closed her eyes.

"It is when it gets in the way of you doing your job." She heard him chuckle.

She could feel him leaning closer to her, could feel his breath on her hair. Opening her eyes, she saw how close he was to her and wanted to lean back, but she didn't. She wasn't going to give him an inch. "In case you've missed it, we are not in the office or sitting in front of a client. What I do, or think about, on my own personal time is my business."

"Come on, Eve, we're friends, right?" He looked at her with his dark eyes and she lost all the pent-up frustration. Why did he always seem to be able to do that?

"Yes, we're friends." She smiled slightly at him.

"Good, why don't you tell your good friend Carter what's bothering you?" He turned his shoulders a little so that his body was facing her. She had always liked his shoulders and the one time she'd actually gotten her hands on them, she hadn't wanted to let go. Her mind flashed to the party he'd thrown for their graduation at his grandparents' place in Maine. She'd been wearing her favorite black bikini, and he'd been in his red swim shorts and no shirt. He'd been wet like he'd just come out of the water, and she'd wanted nothing more than to lick the water drops from every inch of him.

Then Susan had taken that picture of them kissing. It had taken almost three months for Eve to wrangle the negatives out of her. Her only regret was not getting it before Carter had gotten a copy. Knowing he had a copy of that photo only ate her up more. They never spoke of the kiss or the photo. The negative and picture sat in a box in her closet. But the fact that it was there, looming between them, did something to her.

"What?" He looked at her and she watched the small crease creep between his eyebrows. He had nice eyebrows, too. Actually, he had nice everything. His dark hair was always cut short, and his skin was always dark and tan due to his Greek heritage. He was tall and lean with just the amount of muscle tone that made a girl's mouth water. His dark eyes usually told his emotions before his face did. His lips were intoxicating. Her eyes traveled over him as they sat there. Then, with a jerk, the plane started rushing towards the end of the runway and she faced forward and gripped the armrests.

"Still get nervous when you fly?" He chuckled a little.

"Shut up." She closed her eyes and ran through her prayers, ending on a Hail Mary when she felt the vessel level off in the air.

"You've gotten better." When she looked, he was smiling at her. "You used to pray the entire flight."

"Well, I've been flying a lot more lately." She leaned over and removed her tablet and pulled her seat tray down. When she pulled out the small keyboard, she heard Carter sigh.

"What?" She looked at him.

"You don't have to work all the time, you know." He was frowning at her computer.

"I know. I just had a few emails I needed to send before we land." She clicked a few buttons and waited for the screen to pop up.

"They can wait. It's not like your boss is going to fire you, you know." He smiled again and this time, she smiled back.

"I've been meaning to ask you…" She turned towards him, a new plan firmly in her mind. For the past three weeks, since Mitchell had announced he was getting married, she'd been trying to convince them to bring her on as partner. She'd saved enough money in the last five years to buy into the business and wanted nothing more than to be a full partner. But every time she brought it up, Mitch would tell her to talk to Carter, since he was the business head and Mitchell was just the talent scout. Or so he claimed. When she tried to talk to Carter about it, somehow, he always found a way out of the conversations.

Looking around the plane, she doubted he could fake a last-minute business meeting here. Since he was cornered, she decided it was an excellent place to ask about buying in.

"Have you thought about me buying into K&E? Did you look over the business plan I gave you?" She waited for his answer.

"Umm," he looked around, no doubt trying to find the nearest escape.

"Here," she leaned over and pulled a black folder from her

bag and handed it to him. "I bought a copy of my proposal with me."

He looked at the folder in her hands and closed his eyes, faking a snore.

"You can't get away from me this time." She laughed. "Just look over it. It's not like I'm asking much. You know very well that I deserve this chance." She tossed the folder into his lap and watched him pick it up.

"I've already looked it over." He tried to hand it back to her.

"And?" She crossed her arms over her chest.

"And it's a solid business plan." He set the folder on top of her tablet on the tray in front of her.

"That's it?" She held up the folder again. "Solid?"

"Okay, it's a very solid business plan." He smiled at her and crossed his arms, mocking her.

"Carter, just tell me if you don't want me to be a partner. I won't be offended." She set the folder down.

"That's not it." He frowned at her.

"What is it, then? Is my offer too low?" She opened the folder and started looking through her proposal.

"No, if anything it's too much." He looked away.

"What is it, then?" She punched out each word between gritted teeth.

He closed his eyes and sighed. "Listen, how about we grab some dinner tonight and talk about it. I know this great pizza place downtown."

She looked at him. They'd had plenty of dinners together over the years. After all, wining and dining someone was a big part of winning a potential client over. But never had he asked her to dinner, just her, and in such a casual way.

"Why can't you just talk about it now? It's not like we're going anywhere." She motioned around the almost full plane. She was trying to keep her patience in check. He really could be annoying at times. Ever since she'd first met him in middle school, he'd always had to have his way.

Actually, it was due to their friendship and her friendship with Mitchell, that she'd chosen the career path she had. If it wasn't for them, she doubted she would be living in her large apartment overlooking Central Park. She owed the two of them more than she could repay. But that didn't stop her from wanting to become a partner in their ad agency. She'd worked harder than she'd ever dreamed in the last few years, building their clientele to such a high standard and number that they'd hired on several more employees just to manage all the work.

She watched as Carter leaned his head back. "I was hoping to catch some sleep. I was working until early this morning and wanted to shut down for a while." He closed his eyes and she could see a slight smile on his lips. He was avoiding her again. The question was, was she going to allow him to manipulate her so easily.

"That's fine, but I can't do dinner tonight. I am meeting Simon Thomas for dinner." She leaned back and sighed a little, watching Carter's reaction out of the corner of her eye.

"Simon?" Carter sat up a little. "Why are you meeting Simon Thomas for dinner?" She could feel his eyes boring into the side of her face. Closing her eyes a little, it took everything she had not to smile.

"I suppose he wants to talk to me about my proposal." She said easily.

"Proposal?" She heard the anger in his voice and laughed as she opened her eyes and looked at him.

"Really, Carter. Why is it so hard to believe that another ad agency isn't willing to snatch me up? I have a solid proposal. I've proven myself worthy of being a partner. My client lists are impressive, and everyone is happy with my performance. Why are you having such a hard time bringing me in? Even Mitch was on board with my proposal." She glared at him.

He leaned back and looked at her. "Do you really have a meeting with Simon tonight?"

She nodded her head and watched his eyes heat. She knew she'd struck a chord by mentioning Carter's nemesis. But the fact was, Simon had called her up when he'd found out that she'd be in Chicago and had asked her for a meeting. She hadn't sent him a proposal to him, but if Carter didn't give her an answer before they landed; she was seriously thinking about making Simon an offer.

He sat there, silently, and she could tell he was boiling hot. Maybe she had crossed the line a little, but the little cat and mouse game he'd been playing over the last few weeks was tiring. She knew it was time to change who was chasing whom.

Carter stood up and reached into the overhead bin, pulling out his bag. When he sat back down, she could tell he wasn't going to give her an answer.

"Here." He set a large envelope in front of her. "One of the reasons I wanted to do dinner tonight." He set his bag on the ground and leaned back again, closing his eyes.

When she opened the large envelope, she realized she'd misjudged him. There in front of her was all the legal paperwork for her to become a full partner in Kovich & Edwards Agency. All she had to do was sign her name.

She stole a glance at Carter. He was watching her with a large smile on his face. "How about canceling that dinner with Simon Thomas and we'll celebrate with pizza and beer?"

She laughed and smiled at him. "Sounds like a plan, partner."

CARTER RELAXED BACK in his seat and tried not to show his excitement. He'd been upset when Eve had mentioned Simon Thomas's name. The man just got under his skin. Ever since his college days, Simon had followed him around, trying to show him up. Of course, it had helped that Carter had his best friends there, where Simon had always been a loner. When Carter and Mitch started their ad agency fresh from college, Simon had quickly followed suit, using his parents' money to gain some of the best clients around. But a year later, it was Kovich & Edwards Agency that had come out on top. Mitch and Carter had been a dream team, with Carter's business head and Mitchell's ability to spot artistic talent. Not to mention, both of them knew how to treat a client like they were king. The next few years, client after client had left Thomas Ad Agency and signed on with K&E, most of them claiming that lack of communication and the difficulty of working with Simon were the main reasons.

He didn't want Simon Thomas anywhere near Eve, professionally or personally, let alone have her sign on as partner with Thomas Ad Agency.

Carter had looked at Eve's proposal the first night she'd handed it to him and Mitch. He'd spent the whole night reading it over and had an emergency meeting with Mitch the next morning. They would have been stupid not to accept her offer. After all, she was one of the reasons their business had grown so much since they'd brought her on nearly five years ago.

He rested for the remainder of the short trip to Chicago and thought about their dinner plans. The only reason he'd put off making Eve partner was the little leverage he'd had over her. He wasn't a control freak, but he liked knowing she had to come to him for some of the decisions she made. When she was a full partner, he'd miss that. He couldn't deny that she deserved the spot, nor could he deny the attraction he felt for her or the fact that he'd been building up to trying to ask her out. He'd broken up with Lisa, his last girlfriend, only five months ago. It hadn't been one of his longest relationships, only lasting three months. He found it hard to maintain interest in someone ten years his junior when all they wanted to talk about was shopping. He'd called the relationship off, and he'd realized after seeing Mitch and Sandi together that it was time he stepped up and tried for the person he'd always wanted, even if it meant putting himself out there and getting rejected.

His relationship with Eve hadn't always been smooth. A lot of times, they would end their meetings in a fight, usually with Eve winning. The woman knew more tricks to get what she wanted and seemed to always play him for the fool. Not that he minded. Half the time she'd use her sexy hazel eyes on him and he'd lose all his steam. He did enjoy their bantering, often thinking days ahead of how he could win a little tiff he knew was on the way.

He thought about her sitting next to him now and frowned a little. He really had wanted to tell her about the agreement over dinner but hearing her plans with Simon had forced him to play his hand early.

When he felt the plane start to descend, he opened his eyes and found her reading over the agreement he'd had the lawyers draw up. There was a slight frown on her face and a small crinkle between her eyes. She always got that look when she was unhappy about something. She was too busy reading to notice his assessment of her. Her long chestnut hair was tied up in a smart-looking knot at the nape of her neck. Her dark slacks and cream-colored shirt showcased her curvy figure and beautiful olive skin. He and Mitchell always called her Greek Goddess behind her back and the term rang true. But the fact that she could hold her own in a boardroom and sweet talk most clients into anything, gave her the upper edge in his book.

He concentrated on her ear as she read. Her little silver ball earrings bounced as the plane bumped as it landed. She was so caught up in reading, she didn't freak out as she normally did when a plane was landing.

"You took that one like a pro." He chuckled.

"Hmmm, what?" She looked over at him.

"The landing. You didn't freak out." He watched fear come into her eyes as she looked around.

"We've landed?" Upon seeing her grip, the folder tightly, he laughed.

It took a little over an hour to get out of O'Hare and into a taxi heading to their hotel downtown. It was just after noon, so the traffic set them back another hour. He knew she wanted to talk about the paperwork and was surprised that she didn't bring it up. Instead, she looked out the window in deep thought. He had a few loose ends to tie up on his phone and stayed busy most of the taxi ride.

When they arrived at the hotel, Eve checked in and then waited for him in the lobby. He could tell she was deep in thought because when they started walking towards the elevators, he threw her bag over his shoulder and she didn't object. He'd known her since the fourth grade, and she'd never allowed anyone to carry anything for her or to even open the door for her. She was very independent and made sure to let everyone know she could take care of herself.

He supposed it stemmed from being raised by her father. Eve came from a very strict military family. Her father was commanding officer at Fort Drum, a base in upstate New York. Eve never really had anyone to watch out for her. Even now, her family didn't really have a lot to do with her life. Even when they were kids, Eve had pretty much been on her own. He supposed that's why he and Mitch had become such close friends with her. The three of them were pretty much left to their own devices growing up.

Carter was the only one out of the bunch that had family, but after his grandparents died, that had gone away. His mother and father had divorced when Carter was young. He could only remember seeing his dad a handful of times. His mother had always been off somewhere. She'd been in South Africa helping towns build wells when she'd gotten sick. He loved that his mom had such a big heart. He just wished she would have used it closer to home a little more often.

But he'd had his friends and that's all he'd ever needed. Even now, holidays were spent with them, a tradition they'd started in high school. It was just common knowledge that no matter where they were, they'd come together and be there for one another.

He smiled at Eve as they entered the elevator. She'd been like a sister to him until she hadn't. He supposed it was all his fault, really. That kiss had been rolling around in his head for years before he'd acted on it. Since then, their relationship had changed. Not by much, but things were different. He couldn't really put his finger on it, but the sexual tension had tripled between them, especially after her break up with Steve. He knew she'd tried dating shortly after the breakup, each time ending badly. She'd come to her friends for support, and eventually turned to her work to fill the emptiness. A lot like he'd done over the course of the years while she'd been engaged.

He'd tried dating as well. Lisa, for example. Each time had ended just as badly as Eve's relationships had. Actually, now that he thought about it, this was the first time they were both single at the same time.

He watched Eve as she chewed her bottom lip and knew she had something on her mind. "What?" He leaned against the elevator wall.

"What?" She looked at him, trying to fake innocence in her eyes.

"You can't pretend nothing is on your mind. You're dying to get something off your chest." The elevator door opened on their floor. He picked up their bags and they walked out together. He'd arranged it so his room was right next to hers, so when she entered her door, he tried to follow her in.

She slapped her arm across the door and glared at him. "I can take it from here." She held out her hand for her bag.

"I know you can but seeing as you have something you want to get off your chest, we might as well hash it out now." She looked at him and he could see her change her mind, her eyes soften a little. Smiling, he ducked under her arm and walked into her room and set her bag down.

SECRET PASSIONS

DIGITAL ISBN: 978-1-942896-38-8

PRINT ISBN: 978-1-942896-39-5

Copyright © 2013 Grayton Press

All rights reserved.

Copyeditor: Erica Ellis – inkdeepediting.com

Wild Bride

Corey's Catch

Tessa's Turn

The Grayton Series

Last Resort

Someday Beach

Rip Current

In Too Deep

Swept Away

High Tide

Lucky Series

Unlucky In Love

Sweet Resolve

Best of Luck

A Little Luck

Silver Cove Series

Silver Lining

French Kiss

Happy Accident

Hidden Charm

A Silver Cove Christmas

Entangled Series – Paranormal Romance

The Awakening

The Beckoning

The Ascension

Haven, Montana Series

Closer to You

Never Let Go

Holding On

Pride Oregon Series

A Dash of Love

My Kind of Love

Season of Love

Tis the Season

Dare to Love

Where I Belong

Wildflowers Series

Summer Nights

Summer Heat

Stand Alone Books

Twisted Rock

For a complete list of books:

http://JillSanders.com

ABOUT THE AUTHOR

Jill Sanders is a New York Times, USA Today, and international bestselling author of Sweet Contemporary Romance, Romantic Suspense, Western Romance, and Paranormal Romance novels. With over 55 books in eleven series, translations into several different languages, and audiobooks there's plenty to choose from. Look for Jill's bestselling stories wherever romance books are sold or visit her at jillsanders.com

Jill comes from a large family with six siblings, including an identical twin. She was raised in the Pacific Northwest and later relocated to Colorado for college and a successful IT career before discovering her talent for writing sweet and sexy page-turners. After Colorado, she decided to move south, living in Texas and now making her home along the Emerald Coast of Florida. You will find that the settings of several of her series are inspired by her time spent living in these areas. She has two sons and off-set the testosterone in her house by adopting three furry little ladies that provide her company while she's locked in her writing cave. She enjoys heading to the beach, hiking, swimming, wine-tasting, and pickleball with her husband, and of course writing. If you have read any of her books, you may also notice that there is a love of food, espe-

cially sweets! She has been blamed for a few added pounds by her assistant, editor, and fans... donuts or pie anyone?

f facebook.com/JillSandersBooks

twitter.com/JillMSanders

BB bookbub.com/authors/jill-sanders